Dawson's Arm Came Across The Doorway And Blocked Her Exit.

He smiled without humor when she stepped back. He closed the door with a snap and turned to her.

"Why?" she asked.

His eyes ran the length of her, from her loosened wavy dark hair to her trim figure and long, elegant legs in the short black dress.

"Maybe I'm tired of playing games," he said enigmatically.

"I want to go to bed, Dawson."

He let out a long, weary sigh and moved closer. "You run. I run. What difference has it made?" he asked.

His hands shot out and caught her shoulders, and held her against the lean warmth of his powerful body. And he kissed her with aching need, his mind yielding to the feel and touch and taste of her. He groaned as he drew her even closer, his mouth parting her soft lips....

Dear Reader,

It's the **CELEBRATION 1000** moment you've all been waiting for, the publication of Silhouette Desire #1000! As promised, it's a very special MAN OF THE MONTH by Diana Palmer called *Man of Ice*. Diana was one of the very first Silhouette Desire writers, and her many wonderful contributions to the line have made her one of our most beloved authors. This story is sure to make its way to your shelf of "keepers."

But that's not all! Don't miss *Baby Dreams*, the first book in a wonderful new series, THE BABY SHOWER, by Raye Morgan. Award-winning author Jennifer Greene also starts a new miniseries, THE STANFORD SISTERS, with the delightful *The Unwilling Bride*. For something a little different, take a peek at Joan Elliott Pickart's *Apache Dream Bride*. And the fun keeps on coming with Judith McWilliams's *Instant Husband*, the latest in THE WEDDING NIGHT series. Our Debut Author promotion introduces you to Amanda Kramer, author of the charmingly sexy *Baby Bonus*.

And you'll be excited to know that there's more **CELEBRATION 1000** next month, as the party continues with six more scintillating love stories, including *The Accidental Bodyguard*, a MAN OF THE MONTH from Ann Major.

Silhouette Desire—the passion continues! Enjoy!

Lucia Macro

Senior Editor

Please address questions and book requests to:
Silhouette Reader Service
U.S.: 3010 Walden Ave., P.O. Box 1325, Buffalo, NY 14269
Canadian: P.O. Box 609, Fort Erie, Ont. L2A 5X3

DIANA PALMER

MAN OF ICE

CELEBRATION 1000

SILHOUETTE *Desire*®
Published by Silhouette Books
America's Publisher of Contemporary Romance

SILHOUETTE BOOKS

ISBN 0-373-76000-0

MAN OF ICE

This edition published by arrangement with Harlequin Books S.A.

® and TM are trademarks of Harlequin Books S.A., used under license.
Trademarks indicated with ® are registered in the United States Patent
and Trademark Office, the Canadian Trade Marks Office and in other
countries.

Printed in U.S.A.

Dear Reader,

I am delighted to participate in **Celebration 1000** for the Silhouette Desire line. This book, *Man of Ice*, is one of my own favorites, the characters having popped up unexpectedly in the middle of my Special Edition novel *Maggie's Dad*. It seemed a shame to leave them there and not resolve their conflict, so I asked for permission to use them in a book of their own. And here they are.

I have enjoyed my years as a Silhouette author more than I can ever express in words. I have had wonderful editors at Silhouette, where we are as much family as we are author and publisher. It is that way with my readers, as well. I am very happy to be included in the Silhouette Desire **Celebration 1000,** in the company of so many talented Silhouette authors. I want to add my thanks to all of you who have written to me this year and haven't yet had answers! I graduated in May, 1995, summa cum laude, with a Bachelor of Arts degree in history from Piedmont College, Demorest, Georgia. Now that I am out of school, I will have time to answer all the nice letters that have been stacking up for so long. Thank you for your patience—and I hope you enjoy *Man of Ice*.

Love,

Diana Palmer

Prologue

Dawson Rutherford hesitated on the front steps of the Mercer home. As the butler held the carved wooden door open for him to enter, he was only absently aware of music and voices and the clink of ice in glasses. He couldn't remember ever feeling so unsure of himself. Would she welcome him? He smiled with cold mockery. When had Barrie Bell, his stepsister, ever welcomed his presence in recent years? She'd loved him once. But he'd killed her feelings for him, as he'd fought to kill all the violent emotions she inspired in him since her mother had married his father.

He pushed a big, lean hand through his short, wavy gold hair, only barely disrupting its neatness. His pale green eyes were thoughtful as he stood there, elegant and dramatically handsome, drawing the gaze of women. But he had eyes for none of them. They called him the "ice man." And it wasn't because he came from a cold country.

Through the open door he could see her on the steps, her long, wavy black hair curling down her bare shoulders, sparkling in a silver dress. He was all she had left since both their parents had died, but she avoided him. He couldn't blame her, now that he knew at last about the other casualty of his turbulent relationship with Barrie; one that he'd only just found out about recently.

He hesitated to go in there, to see her again, to talk to her. They'd argued at their last meeting over the same issue he was going to bring up now. But this time he needed it as an excuse to get her back to Sheridan, Wyoming. He had to undo five years of pain and heartache, to make up to her for what she'd endured. In order to do that he was going to have to face some private demons of his own, as well as the fear he'd taught her to feel. He didn't look forward to it, but it was time to erase the past and start over. If they could...

One

There was a cardinal rule that people who gave parties never invited both Barrie Bell and her stepbrother, Dawson Rutherford, to the same social event. Since the two of them didn't have a lot of mutual friends, and they lived in different states, it wasn't often broken. But every rule had an exception, and tonight, Barrie discovered, was it.

She hadn't really wanted to go out, but Martha and John Mercer, old friends of the Rutherfords who'd taken a interest in Barrie since their move to Tucson, insisted that she needed a diversion. She wasn't teaching this summer, after all, and the part-time job that kept her bank account healthy had just ended abruptly. Barrie needed cheering up and Martha was giving a party that was guaranteed to accomplish it.

Actually it had. Barrie felt brighter than she had in some months. She was sequestered on the steps of the staircase in the hall with two admirers, one who was a bank executive and the other who played guitar with a jazz band. She was wearing a dress guaranteed to raise blood pressures, silver and clinging from its diamanté straps at her lightly tanned shoulders to her ankles, with a long, seductive slit up one side of the skirt. The color of her high heels matched the dress. She wore her long, wavy black hair loose, so that it reached almost to her waist. In her creamy-complexioned, oval face, bright green eyes shone with a happy glitter.

That is, they *had* been shining until she saw Dawson Rutherford come in the front door. Her sophisticated chatter had died abruptly and she withdrew into a shell, looking vulnerable and hunted.

Her two companions didn't connect her stepbrother's entrance with Barrie's sudden change. Not, at least, until a few minutes later when he spotted her in the hall and, excusing himself to his hostess, came to find her with a drink in his hand.

Dawson was more than a match for any man present, physically. Some of them were spectacularly handsome, but Dawson was more so. He had wavy blond hair, cut conventionally short, a deep tan, chiseled, perfect facial features and deep-set pale green eyes at least two shades lighter than Barrie's. He was tall and slender, but there were powerful muscles in that lithe body, which was kept fit from hours in the saddle. Dawson was a multimillion-aire, yet being the boss didn't keep him from helping out on the many ranches he owned. It was nothing unusual to find him cutting out calves for branding on the Wyoming ranches, or helping to drive cattle across the spinifex plains of the several thousand-square-mile station in Australia's Channel Country. He spent his leisure hours, which were very few, working with his thoroughbred horses on the headquarters ranch in Sheridan, Wyoming, when he wasn't buying and selling cattle all over the country.

He was an elegant man, from his hand-tooled leather boots to the expensive slacks and white silk turtleneck shirt he wore with a designer jacket. Everything about him, from his Rolex to the diamond horseshoe ring on his right hand, screamed wealth. And with the elegant good looks, there was a cold, calculating intelligence. Dawson spoke French and Spanish fluently, and he had a degree in business.

Barrie's two companions seemed to shrink when he appeared beside them, a drink cradled in one big, lean hand. He didn't drink often, and never to excess. He was the sort of man who never liked to lose control in any way. She'd seen him lose it just once. Perhaps that was why he hated her so, because she was the only one who ever had.

"Well, well, what was Martha thinking, I wonder, that rules were made to be broken?" Dawson asked her, his deep voice like velvet even though it carried above the noise.

"Martha invited me. She didn't invite you," Barrie said coldly. "I'm sure it was John. He's laughing," she added, her gaze going to Martha's husband across the room.

Dawson followed her glance to his host and raised his glass. The shorter man raised his in acknowledgment and, catching Barrie's furious glare, turned quickly away.

"Aren't you going to introduce me?" Dawson continued, unabashed, his eyes going now to the two men beside her.

"Oh, this is Ted and that's . . . what was your name?" she somewhat abruptly asked the second man.

"Bill," he replied.

"This is my . . . stepbrother, Dawson Rutherford," she continued.

Bill grinned and extended his hand. It was ignored, although Dawson nodded curtly in acknowledgment. The younger man cleared his throat and smiled sheepishly at Barrie, brandishing his glass. "Uh, I need a refill," he said

quickly, because Dawson's eyes were narrowing and there
was a distinct glitter in them.

"Me, too," Ted added and, grinning apologetically at
Barrie, took off.

Barrie glared after them. "Craven cowards," she muttered.

"Does it take two men at once to keep you happy these
days?" Dawson asked contemptuously. His cold gaze ran
down her dress to the low neckline that displayed her
pretty breasts to their best advantage.

She felt naked. She wouldn't have dreamed of wearing
clothing this revealing around Dawson normally. Only the
fact that he'd come to the party unbeknownst to her gave
him the opportunity to see her in this camouflage she
adopted. But she wasn't going to spoil her sophisticated
image by letting him know that his intent regard disturbed her. "There's safety in numbers," she replied with
a cool smile. "How are you, Dawson?"

"How do I look?" he countered.

"Prosperous," she replied. She didn't say anything else.
Dawson had come to her apartment only a few months
ago, trying to get her back to Sheridan to play chaperone
to Leslie Holton, a widow and former actress who had a
piece of land Dawson wanted. She'd refused and an argument had resulted, which led to them not speaking at
all. She'd thought Dawson would never seek her out again
after it. But here he was. And she could imagine that the
widow was still in hot pursuit of him—or so her best
friend Antonia Hayes Long had told her recently.

He took a sip of his drink, but his eyes never left her
face. "Corlie changes your bed every other day, hoping."

Corlie was the housekeeper at Dawson's Sheridan
home. She and her husband Rodge had been in residence
since long before Barrie's mother had married Dawson's
father. They were two of her favorite people and she

missed them. But not enough to go back, even for a visit. "I don't belong in Sheridan," she said firmly. "Tucson is home, now."

"You don't have a home any more than I do," he shot back, his voice cold. "Our parents are dead. All we have left is each other."

"Then I have nothing," she said harshly, letting her eyes speak for her.

"You'd like to think so, wouldn't you?" he demanded with a cold smile. And because the flat statement wounded him, he added deliberately, "Well, I hope you're not still eating your heart out for me, baby."

The accusation made her feel even more vulnerable. Her hands clenched in her lap. In the old days, Dawson had known too well how she felt about him. It was a weapon he'd used against her. She glared at him. "I wouldn't waste my heart on you. And don't call me baby!"

His eyes narrowed on her face and dropped to her mouth, lingering there. "I don't use endearments, Barrie," he reminded her. "Not in normal conversation. And we both remember the last time I used that one, don't we?"

She wanted to crawl under the stairs and die. Her eyes closed. Memories assailed her. Dawson's deep voice, husky with feeling and need and desire, whispering her name with each movement of his powerful body against hers, whispering, "Baby! Oh, God, baby, baby...!"

She made a hoarse sound and tried to get away, but he was too close. He sat down on the step below hers and settled back on his elbow, so that his arm imprisoned her between himself and the bannister.

"Don't run," he chided. "You're a big girl now. It's all right to have sex with a man, Barrie. You won't go to hell for it. Surely you know that by now, with your record."

She looked at him with fear and humiliation. "My record?" she whispered.

"How many men have you had? Can't you remember?"

Her eyes stared straight into his. She didn't flinch, although she felt like it. "I can remember, Dawson," she said with a forced smile. "I've had one. Only one." She actually shivered.

Her reaction took some of the antagonism out of him. He just stared at her, his pale eyes unusually watchful.

She clasped her arms tightly over her breasts and her entire body went rigid from his proximity.

He moved back, just a couple of inches. She relaxed, but only a little. Her posture was still unnatural. He wanted to think she was acting this way deliberately, in an attempt to resurrect the old guilt. But it wasn't an act. She looked at him with eyes that were vulnerable, but even if she cared as much as ever, she was afraid of him. And it showed.

The knowledge made him uncomfortable. More uncomfortable than he usually was. He'd taunted her with her feelings for him for years, until it was a habit he couldn't break. He'd even done it the night he lost his head and destroyed her innocence. He'd behaved viciously to push away the guilt and the shame he felt at his loss of control.

He hadn't meant to attack her tonight, of all times. Not after the argument he'd had with her months ago. He'd come to make peace. But the attempt had backfired. It was the way she was dressed, and the two eager young men sitting like worshipers at her feet, that had enraged him with jealousy. He hadn't meant a word he said, but she wouldn't know that. She was used to having him bait her. It didn't make him feel like a man to punish her for his own sins; it made him sick. Especially now, with what he'd only just found out about the past, and what had happened to her because of him . . .

He averted his eyes to her folded arms. She looked like a whipped child. She'd adopted that posture after he'd seduced her. The image was burned indelibly into his brain. It still hurt, too.

"I only want to talk," he said curtly. "You can relax."

"What could we possibly have to say to each other?" she asked icily. "I wish I never had to see you again, Dawson!"

His eyes bit into hers. "Like hell you do."

She couldn't win an argument with him. It was better not to start one. "What do you want to talk about?"

His gaze went past her, to the living room, where people were laughing and drinking and talking. Happy, comfortable people. Not like the two on the staircase.

He shrugged and took another swallow from the glass before he faced her again. "What else? I want you to come home for a week or two."

Her heart raced. She averted her gaze. "No!"

He'd expected that reaction. He was ready to debate it. "You'll have plenty of chaperones," he informed her. "Rodge and Corlie." He paused deliberately. "And the widow Holton."

She looked up. "Still?" she muttered sarcastically. "Why don't you just marry her and be done with it?"

He deliberately ignored the sarcasm. "You know that she's got a tract of land in Bighorn that I have to own. The only way she'll discuss selling it to me is if I invite her to Sheridan for a few days."

"I hear that she's hanging around the ranch constantly," she remarked.

"She visits regularly, but not overnight," he said. "The only way I can clinch the land deal and get her to go away is to let her spend a few days at the ranch. I can't do that without you."

He didn't look pleased about it. Odd. She'd heard from her best friend, Antonia Long, that the widow was lovely and eligible. She couldn't understand why Dawson was avoiding her. It was common knowledge that she'd chased Powell Long, Antonia's husband, and that she was casting acquisitive eyes at Dawson as well. Barrie had no right to be jealous, but she was. She didn't look at him, because she didn't want him to know for sure just how vulnerable she still was.

"You must like her if you're willing to have her stay at the ranch," she said. "Why do you keep plaguing me to come and play chaperone?"

His pale green eyes met hers. "I don't want her in my bed. Is that blunt enough?"

She flushed. It wasn't the sort of remark he was in the habit of making to her. They never discussed intimate things at all.

"You still blush like a virgin," he said quietly.

Her eyes flashed. "And you're the one man in the world who has reason to know that I'm not!" she said in a harsh, bitter undertone.

His expression wasn't very readable. He averted his eyes to the carpet. After a minute he finished his drink. He reached through the bannister to put the glass on the hall table beyond it.

She pulled her skirt aside as he reached past her. For an instant, his deeply tanned face was on an unnerving level with hers. She could see the tiny mole at the corner of his mouth, the faint dimple in his firm chin. His upper lip was thinner than the lower one, and she remembered with sorrow how those hard lips felt on her mouth. She'd grieved for him for so long. She'd never been able to stop loving him, despite the pain he'd caused her, despite his suspicions, his antagonism. She wondered sometimes if it would ever stop.

He turned sideways on the step, leaning back against the bannister to cross his long legs in front of him. His boots were immaculate, as was the white silk shirt under his open dinner jacket. But, then, he made the most casual clothes look elegant. He was elegant.

"Why don't you get married?" he asked suddenly.

Her eyebrows went up. "Why should I?"

His quiet gaze went over her body, down her full, firm breasts to her narrow hips and long legs. The side slit had fallen open in the position she was sitting, and all too much of her silk-clad leg was visible.

He watched her face very carefully as he spoke. "Because you're twenty-six. In a few more years, it will be more difficult for you to have a child."

A child... A child. The color drained out of her face, out of her eyes. She swallowed a surge of nausea as she remembered the wrenching pain, the fear as she phoned for an ambulance and was carried to the hospital. He didn't know. He'd never know, because she wouldn't tell him.

"I don't want to marry anyone. Excuse me, I have to—"

She tried to get up, but his lean hand shot out and caught her forearm, anchoring her to the steps. He was too close. She could smell the exotic cologne he always wore, feel his breath, whiskey-scented, on her face.

"Stop running from me!" he growled.

His eyes met hers. They were relentless, intent.

"Let me go!" she raged.

His fingers only tightened. He made her feel like a hysterical idiot with that long, hard stare, but she couldn't stop struggling.

He ended the unequal struggle by tugging slightly and she landed back on the steps with a faint thump. "Stop it," he said firmly.

Her eyes flashed at him, her cheeks flushed.

He let go of her arm all at once. "At least you look alive again," he remarked curtly. "And back to normal pretending to hate me."

"I'm not pretending. I do hate you, Dawson," she said, as if she was programmed to fight him, to deny any hint of caring in her voice.

"Then it shouldn't affect you all that much to come home with me."

"I won't run interference for you with the widow. If you want that land so badly…"

"I can't buy it if she won't sell it," he reminded her. "And she won't sell it unless I entertain her."

"It's a low thing to do, to get a few acres of land."

"Land with the only water on the Bighorn property," he reminded her. "I had free access when her husband was alive. Now I buy the land or Powell Long will buy it and fence it off from my cattle. He hates me."

"I know how he feels," she said pointedly.

"Do you know what she'll do if you're not there?" he continued. "She'll try to seduce me, sure as hell. She thinks no man can resist her. When I refuse her, she'll take her land straight to Powell Long and make him a deal he can't refuse. Your friendship with Antonia won't stop him from fencing off that river, Barrie. Without water, we'll lose the property and all the cattle on it. I'll have to sell at a loss. Part of that particular ranch is your inheritance. You stand to lose even more than I do."

"She wouldn't," she began.

"Don't kid yourself," he drawled. "She's attracted to me. Or don't you remember how that feels?" he added with deliberate sarcasm.

She flushed, but she glared at him. "I'm on vacation."

"So what?"

"I don't like Sheridan, I don't like you, and I don't want to spend my vacation with you!"

"Then don't."

She hit the bannister helplessly. "Why should I care if I lose my inheritance? I've got a good job!"

"Why, indeed?"

But she was weakening. Her part-time job had fallen through. She was looking at having to do some uncomfortable budgeting, despite the good salary she made. It only stretched so far. Besides, she could imagine what a woman like Mrs. Holton would do to get her claws into Dawson. The widow could compromise him, if she didn't do anything else. She could make up some lurid tale about him if he didn't give out . . . and there was plenty of gossip already, about Dawson's lack of interest in women. It didn't bear thinking about, what that sort of gossip would do to Dawson's pride. He'd suffered enough through the gossip about his poor father and Antonia Long, when there wasn't one shred of truth to it. And in his younger days, his success with women was painfully obvious to a worshiping Barrie.

"For a few days, you said," she began.

His eyebrows lifted. "You aren't changing your mind!" he exclaimed with mock surprise.

"I'll think about it," she continued firmly.

He shrugged. "We should be able to live under the same roof for that long without it coming to bloodshed."

"I don't know about that." She leaned against the bannister. "And if I decide to go—which I haven't yet—when she leaves, I leave, whether or not you've got your tract of land."

He smiled faintly. There was something oddly calculating in his eyes. "Afraid to stay with me, alone?"

She didn't have to answer him. Her eyes spoke for her.

"You don't know how flattering that reluctance is these days," he said, searching her eyes. "All the same, it's misplaced. I don't want you, Barrie," he added with a mocking smile.

"You did, once," she reminded him angrily.

He nodded. His hands went into his pockets and his broad shoulders shifted. "It was a long time ago," he said stiffly. "I have other interests now. So do you. All I want is for you to run interference for me until I can get my hands on that property. Which is to your benefit, as well," he added pointedly. "You inherited half the Bighorn property when George died. If we lose the water rights, the land is worthless. That means you inherit nothing. You'll have to depend on your job until you retire."

She knew that. The dividend she received from her share of cattle on the Bighorn ranch helped pay the bills.

"Oh, *there* you are, Dawson, dear!" a honied voice drawled behind him. "I've been looking just everywhere for you!" A slinky brunette, a good few years younger than Barrie, with a smile the size of a dinner plate latched onto Dawson's big arm and pressed her ample, pretty chest against it. "I'd just love to dance with you!" she gushed, her eyes flirting outrageously with his.

Dawson went rigid. If Barrie hadn't seen it for herself, she wouldn't have believed it. With a face that might have been carved from stone, he released himself from the woman's grasp and moved pointedly back from her.

"Excuse me. I'm talking to my stepsister," he said curtly.

The woman was shocked at being snubbed. She was beautiful and quite obviously used to trapping men with that coquettish manner, and the handsomest man here looked at her as if she smelled bad.

She laughed a little nervously. "Of course. I'm sorry. I didn't mean to interrupt. Later, perhaps, then?"

She turned and went quickly back into the living room.

Barrie was standing where she'd been throughout the terse exchange, leaning against the bannister. Now she moved away from it and down the steps to stand just in front of Dawson. Her green eyes searched his quietly.

His jaw clenched. "I told you. I'm not in the market for a woman—not you or anyone else."

Her teeth settled into her lower lip, an old habit that he'd once chided her about.

He apparently hadn't forgotten. His forefinger tapped sharply at her upper lip. "Stop that. You'll draw blood," he accused.

She released the stinging flesh. "I didn't realize," she murmured. She sighed as she searched his hard face. "You loved women, in the old days," she said with more bitterness than she knew. "They followed you around like bees on a honey trail."

His face was hard. "I lost my taste for them."

"But, why?"

"You don't have the right to invade my privacy," he said curtly.

She smiled sadly. "I never did. You were always so mysterious, so private. You never shared anything with me when I was younger. You were always impatient to get away from me."

"Except once," he replied shortly. "And see where that got us."

She took a step toward the living room. "Yes."

There was a silence, filled by merry voices and the clink of ice in glasses.

"If I ask you something, point-blank, will you answer me?" he asked abruptly.

She turned, her eyes wide, questioning. "That depends on what it is. If you won't answer personal questions, I don't see why I should."

His eyes narrowed. "Perhaps not."

She grimaced. "All right. What do you want to know?"

"I want to know," he said quietly, "how many men you've really had since me."

She almost gasped at the audacity of the question.

His eyes slid down her body and back up again, and they were still calculating, the way they'd been all evening. "You dress like a femme fatale. I can't remember the last time I saw you so uncovered. You flirt and tease, but it's all show, it's all on the surface." He scowled. "Barrie..."

She flushed. "Stop looking into my mind! I hated it when I was in my teens and I hate it now!"

He nodded slowly. "It was always like that. I even knew what you were thinking. It was a rare kind of rapport. Somewhere along the way, we lost it."

"You smothered it," she said correcting.

He smiled coolly. "I didn't like having you inside my head."

"Which works both ways," she agreed.

He reached out and touched her cheek lightly, his fingers lingering against the silky soft skin. She didn't move away. That was a first.

"Come here, Barrie," he invited, and this time he didn't smile. His eyes held hers, hypnotized her, beckoned her.

She felt her legs moving when she hadn't meant to let them. She looked up at him with an expression that wasn't even recognizable.

"Now," he said softly, touching her mouth. "Tell me the truth."

She started to clamp down on her lower lip, and his thumb prevented her. It smoothed over her soft lower lip, exploring under the surface, inside where the flesh was moist and vulnerable . She jerked back from him.

"Tell me." His eyes were relentless. She couldn't escape. He was too close.

"I...couldn't, with anyone else," she whispered huskily. "I was afraid."

The years of bitterness, of blaming her for what he thought he'd made of her were based on a lie. All the guilt and shame when he heard about her followers, when he saw her with other men—he knew the truth now. He'd destroyed her as a woman. He'd crippled her sexually. And just because, like his father, he'd lost control of himself. He hadn't known what she'd suffered until a week ago.

He couldn't tell her that he'd wrangled this invitation from John because he needed an excuse to see her. He hadn't realized in all the long years how badly he'd damaged her. Her camouflage had been so good. Now that he did know, it was unbelievably painful.

"Dear God," he said under his breath.

His hand fell away from her cheek. He looked older, suddenly, and there was no mockery in his face now.

"Surprised?" she taunted unsteadily. "Shocked? You've always wanted to think the worst of me. Even that afternoon at the beach, before it . . . before it happened, you thought I just wanted to show off my body."

He didn't blink. His eyes searched hers. "The only eyes you wanted on your body were mine," he said in a dead voice. "I knew it. I wouldn't admit it, that's all."

She laughed coldly. "You said plenty," she reminded him. "That I was a tramp, that I was so hot I couldn't—"

His thumb stopped the words and his eyes closed briefly. "You might not realize it, but you aren't the only one who paid dearly for what happened that night," he said after a minute.

"Don't tell me you were sorry, or that you felt guilty," she chided. "You don't have a heart, Dawson. I don't think you're even human!"

He laughed faintly. "I have doubts about that myself these days," he said evenly.

She was shaking with fury, the past impinging on the present as she struggled with wounding memories. "I loved you!" she said brokenly.

"Dear God, don't you think I know?!" he demanded, and his eyes, for that instant, were terrible to look into.

She went white, paper white. Beside her skirt, her hands clenched. She wanted to throw herself at him and hit him and kick him, to hurt him as he'd hurt her.

But slowly, as she remembered where they were, she forced herself to calm down. "This isn't the time or the place." She bit off the words. Her voice shook with emotion.

He stuck his hands into his pockets and looked down at her. "Come to Wyoming with me. It's time you got it all out of your system. You've been hurt enough for something that was never your fault to begin with."

The words were surprising. He was different, somehow, and she didn't understand why. Even the antagonism when he saw her had been halfhearted, as if he was only sniping at her out of habit. Now, he wasn't especially dangerous at all. But she didn't, couldn't, trust him. There had to be more to his determination to get her to Wyoming than as a chaperone.

"I'll think about it," she said shortly. "But I won't decide tonight. I'm not sure I want to go back to Sheridan, even to save my inheritance."

He started to argue, but the strain of the past few minutes had started to show in her face. He hated seeing the brightness gone from it. He shrugged. "All right. Think it over."

She drew in a steadying breath and walked past him into the living room. And for the rest of the evening, she was the life and soul of the party. Not that Dawson noticed. A couple of minutes after she left him in the hall, he went out the door and drove back to his hotel. Alone.

Two

It was a boring Saturday. Barrie had already done the laundry and gone to the grocery store. She had a date, but she'd canceled it. Somehow, one more outing with a man she didn't care about was more than she could bear. No one was ever going to measure up to Dawson, anyway, as much as she'd like to pretend it would happen. He owned her, as surely as he owned half a dozen ranches and a veritable fleet of cars, even if he didn't want her.

She'd given up hoping for miracles, and after last night, it was obvious that the dislike he'd had for her since her fifteenth birthday wasn't going to diminish. Even her one memory of him as a lover was nothing she wanted to remember. He'd hurt her, and afterwards, he'd accused her of being a wanton who'd teased him into seducing her. He could be kind to the people he liked, but he'd never liked Barrie or her mother. They'd been the outsiders, the interlopers, in the Rutherford family. Barrie's mother had married his father, and Dawson had hated them both from the moment he laid eyes on them.

Eleven years later, after the deaths of both their parents, nothing had changed except that Barrie had learned self-preservation. She'd avoided Dawson like the plague, until last night, when she'd betrayed everything to him in that burst of anger. She was embarrassed and ashamed this morning to have given herself away so completely. Her one hope was that he was already on his way back to Sheridan, and that she wouldn't have to see him again until the incident was forgotten, until these newest wounds he'd inflicted were healed.

She'd just finished mopping the kitchen floor in her bare feet and had put the mop out on the small balcony of her apartment to dry when the doorbell rang.

It was almost lunchtime and she was hungry, having spent her morning working. She hoped it wasn't the man she'd turned down for a date that evening, trying to convince her to change her mind.

Her wavy black hair lay in disheveled glory down her back. It was her one good feature, along with her green eyes. Her mouth was shaped like a bow and her nose was straight, but she wasn't conventionally pretty, although she had a magnificent figure. She was dressed in a T-shirt and a pair of worn jeans. Both garments had shrunk, emphasizing her perfect body. She didn't have makeup on, but her eyes were bright and her cheeks were rosy from all her exertions.

Without thinking, she opened the door and started to speak, when she realized who was standing there. It definitely wasn't Phil, the salesman with whom she'd turned down a date.

It was always the same when she came upon Dawson unawares. Her heart began to race, her breath stilled in her throat, her body burned as if she stood in a fire.

Eyes two shades lighter green than her own looked back at her. Whatever he wore, he looked elegant. He was in designer jeans and a white shirt, with a patterned gray jacket worn loose over them. His feet were encased in hand-tooled gray leather boots and a creamy Stetson dangled from one hand.

He looked her up and down without smiling, without expression. Nothing he felt ever was allowed to show, while Barrie's face was as open as a child's book to him.

"What do you want?" she asked belligerently.

An eyebrow jerked over amused green eyes. "A kind word. But I've given up asking for the impossible. Can I come in? Or," he added, the smile fading, "isn't it convenient?"

She moved away from the door. "Check the bedroom if you like," she said sarcastically.

He searched her eyes. Once, he might have taken her up on it, just to irritate her. Not since last night, though. He hadn't the heart to hurt her any more than he already had. He tossed his hat onto the counter and leaned against it to watch her close the door.

"Have you decided whether or not you'll come back to Sheridan?" he asked bluntly. "It's only for a week. You're on summer vacation, and John told me that you'd been laid off at your part-time job." He looked at the counter and said with calculation, "Surely you can survive without your flock of admirers for that long."

She didn't contradict him or fly off the handle. That was what he wanted. She made points with Dawson by remaining calm.

"I don't want to play chaperone for you, Dawson," she said simply. "Get someone else."

"There isn't anyone else, and you know it. I want that land. What I don't want is to give Mrs. Holden any opportunities for blackmail. She's a lady who's used to getting what she wants."

"You're evenly matched, then, aren't you?" she replied.

"I don't have everything I want," he countered. His eyes narrowed. "Corlie and Rodge will be in the house, too. They miss you."

She didn't answer. She just looked at him, hating him and loving him while all the bad memories surfaced.

"Your eyes are very expressive," he said, searching them. There was so much pain behind the pretense, he thought sadly, and he'd caused it. "Such sad eyes, Barrie."

He sounded mysterious, broody. She sensed a change in him, some ripple of feeling that he concealed, covered up. His lean fingers toyed with the brim of his Stetson and he studied it while he spoke. "I bought you a horse."

She stared at him. "Why?"

"I thought you might respond to a bribe," he said carelessly. "He's a quarter horse. A gelding." He smiled with faint self-contempt. "Can you still ride?"

"Yes." She didn't want to admit that it touched her to have Dawson buy her a present. Even a plastic necklace would have given her pleasure if he'd given it to her.

His eyes lifted back to hers. "Well?"

"You have Rodge and Corlie to play chaperone. You don't need me."

His pale eyes held hers. "Yes, I do. More than you know."

She swallowed. "Look, Dawson, you know I don't want to come back, and you know why. Let's just leave it at that."

His eyes began to glitter. "It's been five years," he said coldly. "You can't live in the past forever!"

"The devil I can't!" she snapped. Her eyes hated him. "I won't forgive you," she whispered, almost choking on the words. "I won't ever, ever forgive you!"

His gaze fell, and his jaw clenched. "I suppose I should have expected that. But hope springs eternal, don't they say?" He picked up his hat and turned back to her.

She hadn't gotten herself under control at all. Her slender hands were clenched at her sides and her eyes blazed.

He paused just in front of her. At close range, he was much taller than she was. And despite their past, his nearness disturbed her. She took a step backward.

"Do you think I don't have scars of my own?" he asked quietly.

"Men made of ice don't get scars," she managed to say hoarsely.

He didn't say another word. He turned and went toward the door. This wasn't like Dawson. He was giving up without a fight; he didn't even seem bent on insulting her. The very lack of retaliation was new and it disturbed her enough to call to him.

"What's wrong?" she asked abruptly, even as he reached for the doorknob.

The question, intimating concern, stopped him in his tracks. He turned as if he didn't really believe she'd asked that. "What?"

"I asked what was wrong," she repeated. "You aren't yourself."

His hand tightened on the doorknob. "How the hell would you know whether I am or not?" he returned.

"You're holding something back."

He stood there breathing roughly, glaring at her. He shifted, restless, as highly strung as she remembered him. He was a little thinner these days, fine-drawn. His eyes narrowed on her face.

"Are you going to tell me?" she asked him.

"No," he said after a minute. "It wouldn't change anything. I don't blame you for wanting to stay away."

He was hiding something. She knew instinctively that he didn't want to tell her. He seemed vulnerable. It shocked her into moving toward him. The action was so unexpected, so foreign, that it stilled his hand on the doorknob. Barrie hadn't come toward him in five years.

She stopped an arm's length away and looked up at him. "Come on, tell me," she said gently. "You're just like your father, everything has to be dragged out of you. Tell me, Dawson."

He took a deep breath, hesitated, and then just told her.

She didn't understand at first.

"You're what?" she asked.

"I'm impotent!"

She just looked at him. So the gossips weren't talking about a cold nature when they called him the "ice man." They were talking about a loss of virility. She hadn't really believed the rumors she'd heard about him.

"But...how...why?" she asked huskily.

"Who knows?" he asked irritably. "What difference does it make?" He took off his hat and ran a lean hand through his hair. "Mrs. Holton is a determined woman, and she thinks she's God's gift to manhood." His face clenched and he averted it, as if it tormented him to tell her all of it. "I need that damn tract of land, but I have to let her come to Sheridan to talk to me about selling it. She wants me, and she'll find out, if she pushes hard enough, that I'm...incapable. Right now it's just gossip. But she'd make me the news item of the century. Who knows? Maybe that's her real reason for wanting to come in the first place, to check out the gossip."

Barrie was horrified. She moved back to the sofa and sat down, hard. Her face was drawn and pale, like his. It shocked her that he'd tell her such a thing, when she was his worst enemy. It was like offering an armed, angry man a bullet for his gun.

He saw her expression and grew angry. "Say something."

"What could I possibly say?" she whispered.

"So you do have some idea of how devastating it is," he murmured from a rigid face.

She folded her hands in her lap. "Then I'm to run interference for you? Will the threat of a sister stop her?"

"That isn't how you'd come back to Sheridan."

She lifted both eyebrows. "How, then?"

He fished a small velvet box out of his pocket and tossed it to her.

She frowned as she opened it. There were two rings inside, a perfect emerald in a Tiffany setting and a matching wedding band set with diamonds and emeralds.

She actually gasped, and dropped the box as if it were red-hot.

He didn't react, although a shadow seemed to pass over his eyes. "Well, that's a novel way of expressing your feelings," he said sardonically.

"You can't be serious!"

"Why can't I?"

"We're related," she blurted out, flushing.

"Like hell we are. There isn't one mutual relative between us."

"People would talk."

"People sure as hell would," he agreed, "but not about my . . . condition."

She understood now, as she hadn't before, exactly what he wanted her to do. He wanted her to come back to Sheridan and pretend to be engaged to him, to stop all the gossip. Most especially, he wanted her there to run interference while Mrs. Holton was visiting, so that she wouldn't find out the truth about him in a physical way while he tried to coax her into selling him that vital piece of land. He could kill two birds with one stone.

To think of Dawson as impotent was staggering. She couldn't imagine what had caused it. Perhaps he'd fallen in love. There had been some talk of him mooning over a woman a few years ago, but no name was ever mentioned.

"How long ago did it happen?" she asked without thinking.

He turned and his green eyes were scorching. "That's none of your business."

Her eyebrows arched. "Well, excuse me! Exactly who's doing whom the favor here?"

"It doesn't give you the right to ask me intimate questions. And it isn't as if you won't benefit from getting her to sell me the land."

She flushed and averted her face.

He rammed his hands into his pockets with an angry murmur. "Barrie, it hurts to talk about it," he snapped.

She should have realized that. A man's ego was a surprisingly fragile thing, and if what she'd read and heard was correct, a large part of that ego had to do with his prowess in bed.

"But you could...you did...with me," she blurted out.

He made a rough sound, almost a laugh. "Oh, yes." He sounded bitter. "I did, didn't I? I wish I could forget."

That was surprising. He'd enjoyed what he did to her, or she certainly thought he had. In fact, he'd sounded as if the pleasure was... She shut out the forbidden thoughts firmly.

He bent and retrieved the jewelry box from the floor, balancing it on his palm.

"It's a very pretty set," she remarked tautly. "Did you just buy it?"

"I've had it for...a while." He stared at the box and then shoved it back into his pocket before he looked at her. He didn't ask. He just looked.

She didn't want to go back to Sheridan. She'd learned last night and this morning that she was still vulnerable with him. But the thought of Dawson being made a laughingstock disturbed her. He had tremendous pride and she didn't want that hurt. What if Mrs. Holton did find out about him and went back to Bighorn and spread it around? Dawson might have recourse at law, but what good would that do once the rumors started flying?

She remembered so well the agony her stepfather and Antonia Hayes had suffered over malicious gossip. Dawson must be remembering as well. There was really no way to answer suspicious looks and whispers. He seemed to have had a bad enough time from just the gossip. How would it be for him if everyone knew for certain that he wasn't capable of having sex?

"Barrie?" he prompted curtly.

She sighed. "Only for a week, you said?" she asked, lifting her eyes to surprise a curious stillness in the expression on his lean, handsome face. "And nobody would know about the 'engagement' except Mrs. Holton?"

He studied his boots. "It might have to be in the local papers, to make it sound real." He didn't look at her. "I doubt it would reach as far as Tucson. Even if it did, we could always break the engagement. Later."

This was all very strange and unexpected. She hadn't really had time to think it through. She should hate him. She'd tried to, over the years. But it all came down to basics, and love didn't die or wear out, no matter how viciously a heart was treated. She'd probably go to her grave with Dawson's name on her lips, despite the lost baby he didn't even know about, and the secret grief she'd endured.

"I need my mind examined," she said absently.

"You'll do it?"

She shrugged. "I'll do it."

He didn't say anything for a minute. Then the box came out of his pocket. "You'll have to wear this."

He knelt just in front of her, where she sat on the sofa, and took out the engagement ring.

"But it might not fit . . ."

She stopped in midstatement as he slid the emerald gently onto her ring finger. It was a perfect fit, as if it had been measured exactly for it.

He didn't say a word. He had her hand in his and, as she watched, he lifted it to his mouth and kissed the ring so tenderly that she stiffened.

He laughed coldly before he lifted his eyes to hers, and if there had been any expression in them, it was gone now. "We might as well do the thing properly, hadn't we?" he asked mockingly, and got gracefully to his feet.

She didn't reply. She still felt his warm mouth on her fingers, as if it were a brand. She looked down at the ring, thinking how perfect the emerald was. Such a flawless stone was easily worth the price of a diamond of equal size.

"Is it synthetic?" she asked absently.

"No. It's not."

She traced around it. "I love emeralds."

"Do you?" he asked carefully.

She lifted her eyes back to his. "I'll take good care of it. The woman you originally bought it for, didn't she want it?" she asked.

His face closed up. "She didn't want me," he replied. "And it's a good thing, considering the circumstances, isn't it?"

He sounded angry. Bitter. Barrie couldn't imagine any sane woman not wanting him. She did, emotionally if not physically. But her responses had been damaged, and he hadn't been particularly kind to her in the aftermath of their one intimacy.

Her eyes on the emerald she asked, "Could you, with her?"

There was a cold pause. "Yes. But she's no longer part of my life, or ever likely to be again."

She recognized the brief flare of anger in his deep voice. "Sorry," she said lightly. "I won't ask any more questions."

He turned away, his hands back in his pockets again. "I thought I might fly you up to Wyoming today, if you don't have anything pressing. A date, perhaps."

She stared at his back. It was strangely straight, almost rigid. "I had the offer of a date," she admitted, "but I refused it. That's who I thought you were. He said he wouldn't take 'no' for an answer...."

Just as she said that, an insistent buzz came from the doorbell. It was repeated three times in quick succession.

Dawson went toward it.

"Dawson, don't you dare!" she called after him.

It didn't even slow him down. He jerked open the door, to reveal a fairly good-looking young blond man with blue eyes and a pert grin.

"Hi!" he said pleasantly. "Barrie home?"

"She's on her way out of state."

The young man, Phil by name, noticed the glare he was getting and the smile began to waver. "Uh, is she a relative of yours?"

"My fiancée," Dawson said, and his lips curled up in a threatening way.

"Fi...what?" Phil's breath exploded.

Barrie eased around Dawson. "Hi, Phil!" she said gaily. "Sorry, but it only just happened. See?" She held out her ring finger. Dawson hadn't budged. He was still standing there, glaring at Phil.

Phil backed up a step. "Uh, well, congratulations, I'm sure. I'll, uh, see you around, then?"

"No," Dawson replied for her.

Barrie moved in front of him. "Sure, Phil. Have a nice weekend. I'm sorry, okay?"

"Okay. Congratulations again," he added, trying to make the best of an embarrassing situation. He shot one last glance at Dawson and returned down the hall the way he'd come, very quickly.

Dawson muttered something under his breath.

Barrie turned and glowered up at him. "That was unkind," she said irritably. "He was a nice man. You scared him half to death!"

"You belong to me for the duration of our 'engagement,'" he said tautly, searching her eyes. "I won't take kindly to other men hanging around until I settle something about that tract of land."

She drew in a sharp breath. "I promised to pretend to be engaged to you, Dawson," she said uneasily. "That's all. I don't belong to you."

His eyes narrowed even more, and there was an expression in them that she remembered from years past.

He looked as if he wanted to say more, but he hesitated. After a minute, he turned away.

"Are you coming with me now?" he asked shortly.

"I have to close up the apartment and pack..."

"Half an hour's work. Well?"

She hesitated. It was like being snared in a net. She wasn't sure that it was a good idea. If she'd had a day to think about it, she was certain that she wouldn't do it.

"Maybe if we wait until Monday," she ventured.

"No. If you have time to think, you won't come. I'm not letting you off the hook. You promised," he added.

She let out an angry breath. "I must be crazy."

"Maybe I am, too," he replied. His hands balled into fists in his pockets. "It was all I could think of on the spur of the moment. I didn't plan to invite her. She invited herself, bag and baggage, in front of half a dozen people and in such a way that I couldn't extricate myself without creating a lot more gossip.''

''There must be other women who would agree to pose as your fiancée,'' she said.

He shook his head. ''Not a one. Or didn't the gossip filter down this far south, Barrie?'' he added with bitter sarcasm. ''Haven't you heard? It would take a blowtorch, isn't that what they say? Only they don't know the truth of it. They think I'm suffering from a broken heart, doomed to desire the one woman I can't have.''

''Are they right?'' she asked, glancing at the ring on her finger.

''Sure,'' he drawled sarcastically. ''I'm dying for love of a woman I lost and I can't make it with any other woman. Doesn't it show?''

If it did, it was invisible. She laughed self-consciously. She'd known there were women in Dawson's life for years, but she and Dawson had been enemies for a long time. She was the last person who'd know about a woman he'd given his heart to. Probably it had happened in the years since they'd returned from that holiday in France. God knew, she'd stayed out of his life ever since.

''Did she die?'' she asked gently.

His chin lifted. ''Maybe she did,'' he replied. ''What difference does it make?''

''None, I guess.'' She studied his lean face, seeing new lines in it. His blond hair had a trace of silver, just barely visible, at his ears. ''Dawson, you're going gray,'' she said softly.

''I'm thirty-five,'' he reminded her.

''Thirty-six in September,'' she added without thinking.

His eyes flashed. He was remembering, as she was, the birthdays when he'd gone out on the town with a succession of beautiful women each year. Once Barrie had tried to give him a present. It was nothing much, just a small silver mouse that she'd saved to buy for him. He'd looked at the present with disdain, and then he'd tossed it to the woman he was taking out that night, to let her enthuse over it. Barrie had never seen it again. She thought he'd probably given it to his date, because it was obvious that it meant nothing to him. His reaction had hurt her more than anything in her life ever did.

"The little cruelties are the worst, aren't they?" he asked, as if he could see the memory, and the pain, in her mind. "They add up over the years."

She turned away. "Everyone goes through them," she said indifferently.

"You had more than most," he said bitterly. "I gave you hell every day of your young life."

"How are we going to Sheridan?" she asked, trying to divert him.

He let out a long breath. "I brought the Learjet down with me."

"It's overcast."

"I'm instrument rated. You know that. Are you afraid to fly with me?"

She turned. "No."

His eyes, for an instant, were haunted. "At least there's something about me that doesn't frighten you," he said heavily. "Go and pack, then. I'll be back for you in two hours."

He went out the door this time, leaving her to ponder on that last statement. But she couldn't make any sense of it, although she spent her packing time trying to.

Three

It was stormy and rain peppered the windscreen of the small jet as Dawson piloted it into his private airstrip at Sheridan. He never flinched nor seemed the least bit agitated at the violent storm they'd flown through just before he set the plane down. He was as controlled in the cockpit as he was behind the wheel of a car and everywhere else. When he'd been fighting the storm, Barrie had seen him smile.

"No butterflies in your stomach?" he taunted when he'd taken off his seat belt.

She shook her head. "You never put a foot wrong when the chips are down," she remarked, without realizing that it might sound like praise.

His pale green eyes searched her face. She looked tired and worried. He wanted to touch her cheek, to bring the color back into her face, the light back into her eyes. But it might frighten her if he reached toward her now. He might have waited too late to build bridges. It was a sobering thought. So much had changed in his life in just the past two weeks, and all because of a chance meeting with an old buddy at a reunion and a leisurely discussion about Tucson, where the friend, a practicing physician, had worked five years earlier in a hospital emergency room.

Barrie noticed his scrutiny and frowned. "Is something wrong?"

"Just about everything, if you want to know," he remarked absently, searching her eyes. "Life teaches hard lessons, little one."

He hadn't called her that, ever. She'd never heard him use such endearments to anyone in normal conversation. There was a new tenderness in the way he treated her, a poignant difference in his whole manner.

She didn't understand it, and she didn't trust it.

A movement caught his eye. "Here comes Rodge," he murmured, nodding toward the ranch road, where a station wagon was hurtling toward the airstrip. "Ten to one he's got Corlie with him."

She smiled. "It's been a long time since I've seen them."

"Not since my father's funeral," he agreed curtly. He left the cockpit and lowered the steps. He went down them first and waited to see if she needed help. But she'd worn sneakers and jeans, not high heels. She went down as if she were a mountain goat. She'd barely gotten onto the tarmac when the station wagon stopped and both doors opened. Corlie, small and wiry and gray-haired, held her arms out. Barrie ran into them, hungry for the older woman's warm affection.

Beside her, Rodge shook Dawson's hand and then waited his turn to give Barrie a hug. He was at least ten years older than Corlie, and still dark-headed with a few silver streaks. He was dark-eyed and lean. When he wasn't managing the ranch in Dawson's absence, he kept busy as

Dawson's secretary, making appointments and handling minor business problems.

The two of them had been with the Rutherfords for so long that they were more like family than paid help. Barrie clung to Corlie. She hadn't realized how much she'd missed the woman.

"Child, you've lost weight," Corlie accused. "Too many missed meals and too much fast food."

"You can feed me while I'm here," she said.

"How long are you staying?" Corlie wanted to know.

Before Barrie could answer her and spill the beans, Dawson caught her left hand and held it under Corlie's nose. "This is the main reason she came back," he said. "We're engaged."

"Oh, my goodness," Corlie exclaimed before a shocked Barrie could utter a single word. The older woman's eyes filled with tears. "It's what Mr. Rutherford always prayed would happen, and me and Rodge, too," she added, hugging Barrie all over again. "I can't tell you how happy I am. Now maybe he'll stop brooding so much and smile once in a while," she added with a grimace at Dawson.

Barrie didn't know what to say. She got lost in the enthusiasm of Rodge's congratulations and Dawson's intimidating presence. He must have had a reason for telling them about the false engagement, perhaps to set the stage for Mrs. Holton's arrival. She could ask him later.

Meanwhile, it was exciting to look around and enjoy being back in Sheridan. The ranch wasn't in town, of course, it was several miles outside the city limits. But it had been Dawson's home when she came here, and she loved it because he did. So many memories had hurt her here. She wondered why it was so dear to her in spite of them.

She found herself installed in the back seat of the station wagon with Corlie while Dawson got in under the wheel and talked business with Rodge all the way up to the house.

The Rutherford home was Victorian. This house had been built at the turn of the century, and it replaced a much earlier structure that Dawson's great-grandfather had built. There had been Rutherfords in Sheridan for three generations.

Barrie often wished that she knew as much about her own background as she knew about Dawson's. Her father had died when she was ten, too young to be very curious about heritage. Then when her mother married George Rutherford, who had been widowed since Dawson was very young, she was so much in love with him that she had no time for her daughter. Dawson had been in the same boat. She'd learned a bit at a time that he and his father had a respectful but very strained relationship. George had expected a lot from his son, and affection was something he never gave to Dawson; at least, not visibly. It was as if there was a barrier between them. Her mother had caused the final rift, just by marrying George. Barrie had been caught in the middle and she became Dawson's scapegoat for the new chaos of his life. George's remarriage had shut Dawson out of his father's life for good.

Barrie had tried to talk to Dawson about his mother once, but he'd verbally slapped her down, hard. After that, she'd made sure personal questions were kept out of their conversation. Even today, he didn't like them. He was private, secretive, mysterious.

Rodge took her bags up to her old room on the second floor, and she looked around the hall, past the sliding doors that led to the living room on one side and the study on the other, down to the winding, carpeted staircase. Suspended above the hall was a huge crystal chandelier, its light reflected from a neat black-and-white-tile floor. The interior of the house was elegant and faintly unexpected on a ranch.

"I'd forgotten how big it is," Barrie mused.

"We used to do a lot of entertaining," Corlie reminded her. She glared at Dawson. "Not anymore."

"I'll remember you said that," he replied. "Perhaps we'll throw a party for Mrs. Holton when she gets here."

"That would make a nice change," Corlie said. She winked at Barrie. "But I expect she's going to be something of a nuisance to a newly engaged couple. I'll help run interference."

She smiled and went off to make coffee.

"Oh, dear," Barrie murmured, seeing more complications down the road.

Dawson shoved his hands into his pockets and searched her face. "Don't worry," he said. "It will all work out."

"Will it?" She grimaced. "What if Mrs. Holton sees right through us?"

He moved a little closer, near enough that she could feel the warmth of his body. "Neither of us is used to touching or being touched," he remarked when she stiffened. "That may be awkward."

She remembered how he'd pushed away the woman at the party in Tucson. Barrie was afraid to come that close, but they were supposed to be engaged and it would look unnatural if they never touched each other.

"What are we going to do?" she asked miserably.

He sighed heavily. "I don't know," he said honestly. Slowly his hand went out, and he touched her long, wavy dark hair. His fingers were just a little awkward. "Maybe we'll improve with some practice."

She bit her lower lip. "I . . . hate being touched," she whispered in a rough whisper.

He winced.

She lowered her eyes to his chest. "Didn't you notice, at the party? I had two men at my feet, but did you see how much distance there was between us? It's always like that. I don't even dance anymore . . . !"

His hand withdrew from her hair and fell to his side. "God forgive me," he said miserably. "I don't think I can ever forgive myself."

Her eyes came up, shocked. He'd never admitted guilt, or fault before. Something must have happened to change him. But what?

"We'll have to spend some time together before she gets here," he said slowly. "And get to know each other a little better. We might try holding hands. Just to get used to the feel of each other."

Tentative. Like children on a first date. She wondered why she was being so whimsical, and smiled.

He smiled back. For the first time in recent memory, it was without malice or mockery.

"Antonia said that Mrs. Holton was very attractive," she remarked.

"She is," he agreed. "But she's cold, Barrie. Not physically, but emotionally. She likes to possess men. I don't think she's capable of deep feelings, unless it's for money. She's very aggressive, single-minded. She'd have made a good corporate executive, except that she's lazy."

"Did her husband leave her well-fixed?" she asked curiously.

"No. That's why she's trying to find a man to keep her."

She bristled. "She ought to go back to school and keep herself," she said shortly.

He laughed softly. "That's what you did," he agreed. "You wouldn't even take an allowance from George. Or from me."

She flushed, averting her eyes. "The Rutherfords put me through college. That was more than enough."

"Barrie, I never thought your mother married my father for his money," he said, reading the painful thought in her mind. "She loved him, just as he loved her."

"That wasn't what you said."

His eyes closed. "And you can't forget, can you? I can't blame you. I was so full of hatred and resentment that I lashed out constantly. You were the most easily reachable...and the most vulnerable." His eyes opened again, cold with self-contempt. "You paid for every sin I accused your mother of committing."

"And how you enjoyed making me pay," she replied huskily.

He looked away, as if the pain in her eyes hurt him. "Yes, I did," he confessed bluntly. "For a while. Then we went to the Riviera on holiday with George."

She couldn't think about that. She didn't dare let herself think about it. She moved away from him. "I should unpack."

"Don't go," he protested. "Corlie's making coffee. She'll probably have cake to go with it."

She hesitated. Her big green eyes lifted to his, wary and uncertain.

His face hardened. "I won't hurt you," he said roughly. "I give you my word."

He was old-fashioned that way. If he made a promise, he kept it. But why should he stop sniping at her now, and so suddenly? Her eyes mirrored all her uncertainties, all her doubts.

"What's changed?" she asked miserably.

"*I've* changed," he replied firmly.

"You suddenly woke up one morning and decided that you'd give up an eleven-year vendetta?"

He searched over her face with an enigmatic expression on his darkly tanned face. "No. I discovered how much I'd lost," he said, his voice taut with some buried feeling. "Have you ever thought that sometimes our whole lives pivot on one decision? On a lost letter or a telephone call that doesn't get made?"

"No, I don't suppose I have, really," she replied.

"We live and learn. And the lessons get more expensive with age."

"You're very reflective, lately," she said, curious. A strand of hair fell over her eyes, and she pushed it back from her face. "I don't think in all the time we've known each other that we've really talked, until the past day or so."

"Yes. I know." He sounded bitter. He turned away from her to lead the way into the spacious living room. It had changed since she'd lived on the Rutherford ranch. This was the very room where Dawson had so carelessly tossed the little silver mouse she'd given him to his date. But it wasn't the same at all. The furniture was different, Victorian and sturdy in its look, but wonderful to sink into.

"This room doesn't look like you at all," she remarked as she perched herself in a delicate-looking wing chair that was surprisingly comfortable.

"It isn't supposed to," he replied. He sat down on the velvet-covered sofa. "I hired a decorator to do it."

"What did you tell her, that you wanted to adopt someone's grandmother and install her here?" she asked.

He lifted an eyebrow. "In case you didn't notice, the house is late Victorian. And I thought you liked Victorian furniture," he added.

She shifted, running her hand along the arm of the chair. "I love it," she confessed in a subdued tone. Questions poised on the tip of her tongue, and she almost asked them, but Corlie came in with a tray of cake and coffee, beaming.

"Just what the doctor ordered," she said smugly, putting the tray on the big coffee table.

"Great huge coffee tables aren't Victorian," Barrie muttered.

"Sure they are. Victorians drank coffee," Corlie argued.

"They drank tea," she replied, "and out of dainty little china cups and saucers."

"They also ate cucumber sandwiches," Corlie returned. "Want a few?"

Barrie made a face. "I'll be quiet about the coffee table if you won't offer me those again."

"It's a deal. Call if you need anything else." Corlie went out, closing the sliding doors behind her.

She helped herself to coffee and cake and so did he. As always he took his coffee black while Barrie put cream and sugar in hers.

"Antonia said that you'd been offered a job heading the math department at your high school next fall," he remarked. "Are you going to take it?"

She looked up over the rim of her coffee cup. "I don't know," she replied. "I love teaching. But that job is mostly administrative. It would take away the time I had with my students, and plenty of them require extra tutoring."

He searched her down-bent face. "You...like children, don't you?"

"Oh, yes." She toyed with her coffee cup, trying not to think about the child they'd made, the one she'd lost so many years ago.

He sat, waiting, hoping that she might finally decide to tell him her secrets. But the moment passed. She went right on eating cake and drinking coffee, and she didn't make another remark. He was hesitant about bringing it up himself. They had a long way to go before she might feel comfortable talking about something so intimate and painful with him.

He changed the subject and conversation reverted to impersonal topics. He went into his study to make some phone calls and she went upstairs to unpack.

She wondered at the change in him, but she was still too raw from the past to let her guard down.

Supper was a cheerful affair, with Rodge and Corlie sitting at the table with Barrie and a taciturn Dawson. They talked. He listened. He seemed preoccupied, and he excused himself to work in the study. He didn't come back, even when Barrie said good-night to Corlie and Rodge and went up to her old room to go to bed.

She lay awake for a long time. Being in the house again brought back memories, so many memories, of Dawson and his antagonism. Then, inevitably, her mind went to the Riviera....

It had been a beautiful summer day. Sea gulls had dived and pitched above the white beach where Barrie sat on a big beach blanket and worried about her conservative appearance. Many people were nude. Most of the women were topless. Nobody seemed to pay the least attention, either.

Barrie wanted to sunbathe without white lines, but she was inhibited at twenty-one, and a little intimidated by Dawson in his white trunks. He was exquisite, and she couldn't keep her eyes off him. A thick thatch of curly gold hair, darker than that on his head, covered his broad chest and narrowed down his flat stomach into his trunks. Long, elegantly powerful legs had the same tan as the rest of his body. She imagined that he normally sunbathed without any trunks at all, although she didn't know for sure.

The path of her thoughts embarrassed her and she averted her eyes. But her hands toyed with the ties of her bikini top as she thought daringly how it would be to let it fall, to know that Dawson's gaze was on her bare breasts. She shivered with just the thought of it, and wished she were sophisticated and chic like his usual companions, that she had the nerve just once to do something outrageous and shocking.

She'd glanced at him in what might have seemed a coquettish way as her fingers toyed with the straps and she'd smiled nervously.

Dawson hadn't realized how inhibited she was. He'd formed the idea that Barrie was a born flirt, that she collected men. He'd always seen her shy attempts at affection as deliberate coquetry, because it was the sort of game the sophisticated women he knew played.

So when Barrie had darted that curious glance at him, he'd thought she wanted him to coax her into taking off the top. And because she had a lovely young body, and he wanted very much to look at it, he'd played along.

"Go ahead," he'd murmured in a deep, tender voice. "Untie it, Barrie. I want to look at you."

She remembered looking into his eyes and seeing the lazy sensuality in them, the calculating narrowness of them.

"Why the hesitation?" he'd taunted. "You're drawing attention because you're being so damned conservative. None of the other women have any hang-ups about their bodies."

He nodded toward two young women about Barrie's age, dancing along the beach with only bikini bottoms covering their womanliness.

She bit her lip, hesitating, turned just sideways from him, toward the beach.

He'd been beside her, facing her on his knees, his lean hands resting on his muscular thighs. "Barrie?" he'd coaxed softly. And when she looked at him his voice softened and deepened. "Take it off."

He hypnotized her with forbidden longings, with long-buried needs. Her hands fumbled with the single tie at the back of her neck and she loosened it. Her fingers reached around to the other single fastening under her shoulder blades. She looked into his pale green eyes, trembling with new sensations, flushing at the enormity of what she was doing. And she let the top fall away.

She remembered even now the feel of his eyes, the soft intake of his breath as he'd looked at her. She had high, firm, full breasts, pale pink, with darker pink crowns that went rigid under the impact of his level gaze.

She trembled helplessly as he looked his fill. There was a dark flush along his high cheekbones, and he made no pretence of not staring.

Unexpectedly his eyes lifted to hold hers. Whatever he'd seen there must have told him what he wanted to know, because he'd made a sound deep in his throat and stood up. He seemed to vibrate with some violent emotion. Suddenly he'd bent and slipped his arms under her knees and her back and lifted her off the sand. His eyes stared into hers as he slowly, exquisitely, brought her upper body to his so that her breasts flattened gently in the thick hair that covered his broad chest. His skin was as cool from the breeze as hers was hot from the feelings he aroused in her virginal body. She'd stiffened at the shock of the contact.

"No one is looking," he said roughly. "No one gives a damn. Put your arms around me and come closer."

It was shocking, the need she felt. She obeyed him, forgetting her shyness as she ached to feel his body against hers. She remembered burying her hot face in his throat, drinking in the scent of him, feeling his heavy, harsh pulse against her bare breasts as his arms tightened and he walked toward the water with her.

"Wh . . . why?" She choked.

"Because I'm so damned aroused that I can't hide it," he said half angrily. "The only escape is right into the ocean. Or don't you feel it, too, Barrie? A burning deep in your belly, an emptiness that wants filling, an ache that hurts?"

Her arms contracted and she moaned softly.

"Yes, you feel it," he breathed as he began to wade into the water. His face slid against hers and his mouth suddenly opened as it sought and found her parted lips. She didn't remember the shock of the water. There was nothing in life except that first, burning sweetness of Dawson's hard mouth on her lips, nothing more than the feel of him in her arms, against her bare breasts.

Vaguely she was aware that they were in the warm water, that his arms had released her so that he could pull her into an even more intimate embrace. His long legs tangled with hers, and for the first time, she felt the force of his desire for her. They kissed and kissed, there in the water, oblivious to the whole world, to the line of hotels above the shore, the other swimmers, the noise on the beach.

He moved her, just enough to let his lean hand find and swallow one swollen breast. His tongue eased into her open mouth. His free hand lifted and pulled her, fit her exactly to the hard thrust of him. And she almost lost consciousness at the stabbing ache of pleasure he kindled in her trembling body, there in the water, there in the blue ocean....

She fell asleep with the memories deep in her mind. Unfortunately, those sweet memories merged with some that were much darker. Dawson had finally gained temporary control of himself, and left her alone in the sea to recover from their feverish embraces. But all through the evening meal with George, he'd watched Barrie with eyes that made her feel hunted. The idiotic way she'd smiled at him and encouraged his watchfulness could still make her cringe. She'd thought he was falling in love with her, and she was doing her best to show him that she already felt that way about him. She'd had no idea how he was interpreting her shy flirting.

But it had all become clear after she'd gone to bed that night. The sliding door on her balcony had opened and

Dawson had come through it. He'd been wearing a robe and nothing else. Barrie remembered the sweep of his hand as he tore the sheet away from her body, clad only in thin briefs because of the heat and the failing air-conditioning. Her body had reacted at once to his eyes, and even the shock and faint fear hadn't robbed her of the desire that was all too visible to a man of Dawson's experience.

"Want me, Barrie?" he'd whispered as he threw off his robe and joined her on the bed. "Let's see how well you follow up on those teasing little glances you've been giving me all night."

She hadn't had the presence of mind to explain that she hadn't been teasing him. She wanted to tell him that she loved him, that he was her life. But his hands on her body were shocking, like the things he whispered to her in the moonlight, like the feel of his mouth surging over her taut breasts while he made love to her as if he were some demon of the night.

If she'd been the experienced woman he thought her, it would have been a night to remember. But she'd been a virgin, and he'd been completely out of control. She remembered the faint tremor in the hands that had gathered her hips up to the fierce thrust of his body, his cry of pleasure that drowned out her cry of pain. He whispered to her all through it, his body as insistent as his mouth, his hands, until finally he arched up as though he were on some invisible rack, his powerful body cording with ripple after ripple of ecstasy until he convulsed with hoarse, fierce cries and his hands hurt her.

She felt no such pleasure. Her body felt torn and violated. She was almost sick with the pain that had never seemed to stop. When he pulled away from her finally, exhausted and sweaty, she winced and cried out, because that hurt, too.

She wept, curled into a ball, while he got to his feet and put his robe back on. He'd looked down at her sobbing form with eyes she couldn't see, and she didn't like remembering the things he'd said to her then. His voice had been as brutal as his invasion of her, and she'd been far too innocent to realize that he was shocked and upset by her innocence, hitting out to disguise his own stark guilt. It could have been so different if he'd loved her. But in the darkness of her dream, he was a bird of prey, tearing at her flesh, hurting her, hurting her...

She didn't realize that she'd screamed. She heard the door open and close, felt light against her eyelids, and then felt hands shaking her.

"Barrie. Barrie!"

She came awake with a start, and the face above her was Dawson's. He was wearing a robe, as he had been that night. His hair was damp from a shower, and her mind reverted to the night she'd spent in his arms in France.

"Don't... hurt me... anymore!" she whispered, sobbing.

He didn't reply. He couldn't. The terror in those eyes made him sick right through to his soul. "Dear God," he breathed.

Four

Barrie saw his face contort and as she came back to awareness, she noticed the room around her, the light fixture overhead. "It's...not France," She choked. Her eyes closed. "Oh, thank God, thank God!"

Dawson got up from the bed and moved to the window. He moved the curtain aside and looked out into the darkness. He wasn't looking at anything. He was seeing the past, the horror in Barrie's eyes, the pain that he'd caused.

Barrie sat up. She noticed his lean hand clenching the curtains. It had gone white. He looked beaten, exhausted.

She swallowed hard. Her hands went to her pale cheeks and smoothed over them and then pushed back the tangled dark hair that fell over her breasts. She was wearing a long cotton gown that completely covered her except for her arms and a little of her slender neck. She never slept just in her briefs these days, not even in summer.

"I didn't realize that you still had nightmares about it," he said after a minute. His voice was dull and without expression.

"Not very often," she said. She couldn't tell him that most of them ended with her losing the baby, crying out for Dawson. That hadn't happened tonight, thank God. She couldn't bear for him to know it all.

He turned away from the window and moved back to the side of the bed, but not close. His hands closed in the pockets of his robe.

"It wouldn't be that way a second time," he said stiffly.

Her eyes widened in fear, as if he'd suggested seducing her all over again. The realization infuriated him, but he controlled the surge of anger. "Not... with me." He bit off the words, averting his face. "I didn't mean that."

She drew her knees up and wrapped her arms around them. The sound of the fabric sliding against her skin was abnormally loud. She glanced up at him and the memories began to recede. If she was hurting, so was he. He couldn't fake the sort of pain she saw in his drawn face.

"Haven't you even been curious since then, for God's sake?" he asked. "You're a woman. You must have friends, people you could ask. Surely someone told you that first times are notoriously bad."

She smoothed one hand over the other. Her body slumped with a long sigh. "I can't talk to anyone about it," she said finally. "I only have one best friend. And how could I possibly ask Antonia, when she's known us both for years? She wouldn't need two guesses to figure out why I was asking."

He nodded. "You were a virgin. You needed time to be properly aroused, especially with me, and I lost control much too soon," he added. His eyes searched her face grimly. "That was a first for me. Until you came along, there had never been a woman who could throw me off-balance in bed."

Her face lowered. It was an accomplishment of sorts, she supposed.

"I damaged both of us that night," he said gently. "Until I had you, I genuinely thought you were experienced, Barrie, that you were only teasing on the beach when you had to be coaxed into removing your top."

That brought her eyes up to his, shocked. "But I would never have done such a thing!" she protested.

"I had to find that out the hard way," he replied. "Maybe I used it as an excuse, too. I wanted you and I convinced myself that you'd surely had men at your age, that it had all been playacting on your part, all that coy shyness. But it didn't take me long to realize why you'd given in without a struggle. You loved me," he said huskily.

Her eyes closed. She couldn't bear to hear him say it again. He'd taunted her with her feelings after that disastrous night.

She felt the bed depress as he sat down slowly beside her. His hand tipped her head back toward his, making her look at him. "Guilt will drive a man to violence, Barrie," he said, his voice deep and soft in the silence of her room. "Especially when he's done something unforgivable and knows he'll never find forgiveness for it. I taunted you because I couldn't live with what I'd done to you. It doesn't make much sense, now. But at the time, blaming you was the only thing that kept me from putting a gun to my head."

She hadn't said a word. Her big eyes were locked into his as she struggled to understand him.

"I couldn't stop." He took an unsteady breath. "God, Barrie, I tried. I tried. But I couldn't...stop." He leaned forward, his head down bent, defeated. "For months after it happened, I could hear your voice in my nightmares. I knew I was hurting you, but I couldn't draw back."

She didn't understand desire of that sort, pleasure too blind to feel pity. She'd never felt it, although the way he'd kissed her in the ocean had made her hungry for something. "I wanted you, too."

He lifted his head and looked down at her. "You don't understand, do you?" he asked gently. "You've never felt desire that overwhelming. Your only knowledge of real intimacy is forever embedded in pain."

"I didn't know you had nightmares," she said slowly.

"I still have them," he said on a cold laugh. "Just like you."

Her gaze went over his face like searching hands. "Why did you come to my room that night?" she asked softly.

He moved, one long arm going across her body to support him as he leaned closer, so that his face filled her entire line of vision. "Because I wanted you so much that I would have died to have you," he said through his teeth.

The subdued violence in the flat statement surprised her. Perhaps she'd known on some unspoken level how desperately hungry he'd been for her, but he'd never actually said the words before.

"I wanted you so much that I was almost sick with it. I came to you because I couldn't stop myself. And it does no good whatsoever five years after the fact to tell you that I'm sorry."

"*Are* you sorry?" she asked sadly.

He nodded, without blinking an eye. "Sorry. Bitter. Hurt. All the things you were. But there was more to it than just physical pain on your part." He didn't move. He didn't seem to breathe. He took a slow, deliberate breath. "You never told me that I gave you a baby that night. Or that, several weeks later, you lost it. Did you think I wouldn't find out, someday?" he concluded heavily, the pain lying dark and dull in his eyes as he saw the shock register on her face.

Her heart skipped and ran away. "I...how did you find out?" she faltered. "I never even told Antonia!"

"Do you remember the intern who attended to you in the emergency room?"

"Yes. Richard Dean," she recalled. "He'd been a student in your graduating class. But you never saw him, he even said that you didn't mix socially. Besides, he was a doctor, he took an oath never to talk about his patients...!"

"We met at a class reunion a few weeks ago," he confided. "He thought I knew. You're my stepsister, after all, he reminded me. He assumed that you'd told me."

She gnawed her lower lip, staring up at him worriedly.

His lean hand came to touch her mouth, disturbing the grip of her teeth. "Don't," he said softly.

"I forget sometimes," she murmured.

His thumb traced over her mouth gently. He searched her eyes. "He said...that you were utterly devastated," he whispered. "That you cried until he had to sedate you." His face drew up with bitterness. "He said you wanted the baby desperately, Barrie."

She dragged her eyes down to his chest. "It was a long time ago." Her voice sounded stiff.

He let out a heavy breath. "Yes, and you've done your grieving. But I've only just started. I didn't know until Richard told me. It's been a little rough, losing a child I didn't even know I'd helped create."

His face was averted, but she could see the pain on it. It was the first time they'd really shared grief, except when his father had died. But that had only been a few words, because she couldn't stand to be near him so soon after the Riviera.

"Would you have told me?" he asked, staring at the wall.

"I'm not sure. It seemed senseless, after so long a time. You didn't know about the baby. I wasn't sure you'd want to know."

He caught her slender hand in his and linked his fingers with it. "I got drunk and stayed drunk for three days after I got back from my class reunion," he said after a minute. Then he added, expressionlessly, "Richard said that you asked a nurse to call me from the emergency room."

She stared at the big hand holding hers so closely. "Yes, in a moment of madness."

"I didn't know she was a nurse. She mentioned your name and before she could say why she was calling, I hung up on her."

His fingers had tightened painfully. "Yes," she said.

He drew her hand to his lips and kissed it hungrily.

His head was bent over her hand, but she saw the faint wetness at the corner of his eye and she gasped, horrified.

As if his pride wouldn't take that sort of blow, letting her see the wetness in his eyes, he let go of her fingers and got up, going back to stand at the darkened window. He didn't speak for a full minute, his hand gripping the curtain tightly. "Richard said it was a boy."

She rested her forehead against her knees. "Please," she whispered gruffly. "I can't talk about it."

He moved from the window, back to the bed. He tore the covers away and scooped her up into his arms, sitting down to hold her tight, tight, across his legs, with his face against her soft throat.

"I've got you," he whispered roughly. "You're safe. Nothing will ever hurt you again. Cry for him. God knows I have!"

The tender gruffness in his deep voice broke the dam behind which her tears had hidden. She gave way to them, for the first time since the miscarriage. She wept for the son she'd lost. She wept for her pain, and for his. She wept for all the lost, lonely years.

A long time later, she felt him dabbing at her eyes with a corner of the sheet. She took it from him and finished the job. And still he held her, gently, without passion. Her cheek felt the regular, hard beat of his heart under the soft fabric of the robe. She opened her hot, stinging eyes and stared across at the dark window, all the fire and pain wept out of her in salty tears.

"It's late," he said finally. "Mrs. Holton arrives first thing in the morning. You need to get some sleep."

She stretched, boneless from exhaustion, and looked up into his quiet, watchful eyes. Involuntarily his own gaze went down to the soft thrust of her breasts under the cotton gown. He remembered the beauty of her body, years after his last glimpse of it.

She watched him staring at her, but she didn't move or flinch.

"Don't you want to run?" he taunted.

She shook her head. Her eyes looked straight up into his. She slid her fingers over the lean, strong hand that was lying across her waist. She tugged at it until it lifted. She smoothed it up her side, over her rib cage, and then gently settled it directly over one soft breast.

His intake of breath was audible, and his body seemed to jump.

"No," he said curtly, jerking his hand down to her waist. "Don't be stupid."

She felt less confident than she had before, but there was a faint film of sweat over his upper lip. He was more shaken than he looked.

"Don't make me ashamed. It's hard for me, to even think of this, much less...do it," she said. "I only wanted to know if I could let you touch me," she finished with a rueful smile.

The cold hauteur left him. "I can't take the risk, even if you're willing to." He started to move her aside, but she clung.

"What risk?" she asked.

"Don't you know? You don't need to find out the hard way that I can still want you." He laughed coldly. "I'm not sure I want to know, either."

While she was working that one out, he lifted her and placed her gently onto the pillows. He got up and moved back from the bed. "Go to sleep."

"What if you could . . . want me?" she persisted, levering up on her elbows.

He looked unutterably weary. "Barrie, we both know that you'd scream the minute I touched you with intent," he said. "You couldn't help it. And even if I could feel anything with you, it might be just the way it was before. I might lose my head again, hurt you again."

"I'm not a virgin anymore," she said without thinking.

His face was quiet, expressionless as he looked down at her. "It's a moot point. My body is dead, as far as sex is concerned. For both our sakes, let well enough alone. It's too soon for experimenting."

Before she could speak, he'd gone out the door, closing it behind him with a firm snap. Barrie lay back, turning what he'd said over in her mind.

He knew, finally, about the baby they'd lost. She didn't know if she was sorry or glad, but it had been cathartic to have it all out in the open. He grieved for their child, at least, as she did. But he had nothing to give her, and she still loved him. It was a problem that had no easy resolution, and in the morning a new complication was due to present itself. She wondered how she was going to react to the widow Holton. It would be an interesting introduction, at the very least.

* * *

Leslie Holton blew in the next morning like a redheaded tornado, driving a brand-new shiny black Jaguar. Peering through the lacy curtains in the living room when she drove up, Barrie couldn't help thinking that the car suited her. Mrs. Holton was sleek and dangerous-looking, a powerhouse no less than the car she drove. She was wearing a black-and-white suit. Its starkness made her pale skin even paler and presented a backdrop for her fiery hair. Wickedly Barrie wondered how much of it came out of a bottle, because the widow was obviously over twenty-one. Way over.

She went out into the hall and met up with Dawson who had just come out of his study. There were dark circles under his eyes. He appeared worn, as if he hadn't slept. He looked across at Barrie, and she realized that he hadn't slept at all.

She moved toward him. Last night had calmed some old terrors, the way they'd talked had changed things in some subtle way. She stopped in front of him and looked up.

"You haven't had any sleep," she said gently.

His face hardened. "Don't push your luck."

Her eyebrows lifted. "Am I?"

"Looking at me like that is chancy."

She smiled. "What will you do?" she chided.

Something equally reckless flared in his pale eyes. "Want to see?"

He moved forward with an economy of motion to scoop her up against his chest. He held her there, searching her eyes at point-blank range.

Her arms tightened around his strong neck and she looked back at him curiously. He'd wanted the baby, too. That knowledge had changed the way she envisioned him. Even though there was some residual fear of him in her, the memory of the grief she'd seen in his face last night tempered it.

"Doesn't anybody hear the doorbell ringing?" Corlie muttered as she came out of the kitchen and suddenly spotted Dawson holding Barrie off the floor in his arms. "Well, excuse me." She chuckled, sparing them a wicked glance as she went toward the front door.

Barrie started to speak but Dawson shook his head. "Don't disillusion her," he whispered. "Let her hope."

Something in the way he said it made her look at him curiously. His pale eyes fell to her mouth and he hesitated.

"If you wanted to kiss me, you could," she said boldly. "I mean, I wouldn't scream or anything."

"Cheeky brat," he muttered, but he was still looking at her mouth.

"I can always tell when you've been on a trip to the station in Australia," she whispered.

"Can you?" His head bent closer, his mouth threatening her soft lips. His arms contracted a little. Somewhere in the distance, a stringent voice was demanding that Corlie have someone get luggage out of the Jaguar.

"Yes," she whispered at his lips. "You always come back using Aussie slang."

He chuckled softly.

Barrie felt the vibration of his laughter all the way to her toes. It was the old magic, without the fear. She loved him. His arms were warm and strong and safe, and her hands clasped together behind his neck. She lifted herself closer to that hard, beautiful mouth and parted her lips.

"No self-preservation left, Barrie?" he whispered huskily. His own lips parted and moved down slowly. "Baby," he breathed into her mouth. "Baby, baby...!"

The pressure became slow and soft and insistent. It began to deepen and she caught her breath, anticipating the hunger that she could already taste...

"Dawson!"

Their faces jerked apart. Dawson stared at the new-comer just for a moment with eyes that didn't quite fo-cus. "Leslie," he said then. "Welcome to White Ridge." He lowered Barrie gently to her feet and, keeping a pos-sessive arm around her, held his hand out to Leslie.

Mrs. Holton made an indignant sound. "Hello, Daw-son," she said impatiently. "My goodness, isn't that your stepsister?"

"She was," Dawson replied coolly. "Yesterday, she became my fiancée. We're engaged."

Mrs. Holton was clearly surprised. "But isn't that against the law?"

"Barrie and I aren't blood-related in any way," he said. "My father married her mother."

"Oh." Leslie stared at Barrie, who grinned at her. "I'm glad to meet you, Miss Rutherford."

"Bell," Barrie corrected her, extending a hand. She was quivering inside, all raw nerves and excitement. "Barrie Bell."

"I didn't expect this," Mrs. Holton said. She eyed Dawson carefully. "Of course, it's very sudden, isn't it?" She smiled with feline calculation. "In fact, I seem to re-member hearing that the two of you didn't even speak. When did that change?"

"Yesterday," Dawson said, unperturbed. He looked down at Barrie. "It was sudden, all right. Like a bolt of lightning." His eyes fell to her soft mouth as he said it, and she caught her breath at the surge of feeling the stare provoked.

Leslie Holton wasn't blind, but she was determined. "You do, uh, still want to discuss my tract of land near Bighorn?" she asked with a calculating smile.

"Of course," Dawson replied, and he smiled back. "That was the purpose of your visit, wasn't it?"

She shrugged a thin shoulder. "Well, yes, among other things. I do hope you're going to show me around the ranch while I'm here. I'm very interested in livestock."

"Barrie and I will be delighted, won't we, baby?" he added with a glance at Barrie that made her toes curl.

She pressed close to his side, shocked at her surge of hunger to be near him. It was equally shocking to hear his faint breath and feel his arm tighten around her shoulders.

"Certainly," she said. She smiled at Mrs. Holton, but she sounded, and felt, breathless.

"Corlie will show you to your room, and Rodge will bring your bags right up," Dawson said. "I'll be right back." He let go of Barrie with a smile and went to call Rodge on the intercom.

"You teach, don't you?" Mrs. Holton asked Barrie. "You must be on summer vacation."

"Yes, I am. What do you do?" Barrie shot right back.

"Do? My dear, I'm rich," Leslie said with hauteur. "I don't have to work for a living." Her eyes narrowed with calculation. "And neither will you after you marry Dawson. Is that why you're marrying him?"

"Of course," she murmured wickedly. She glanced at Dawson, who was just coming out of the study again. "Dawson, you do know that I'm only marrying you for your money, don't you?" she asked, raising her voice.

He chuckled. "Sure."

Leslie was confused. She looked from one of them to the other. "What a very odd couple you are."

"You have no idea," Barrie murmured dryly.

"Amen," he added.

"Well, I'll just slip upstairs and rest for a few minutes, if you don't mind," Leslie said. "It's been a long, tiring drive." She paused in front of Dawson and smiled up at him seductively. "I might even soak in the hot tub for a little while. If you'd like to wash my back, you're welcome," she added teasingly.

Dawson didn't reply. He just smiled.

Leslie glowered at him, glanced at Barrie irritably and followed an impatient Corlie up the staircase.

Barrie moved closer to him. "Do we have hot water, or is it still subject to fits of temperament in the spring?"

"We have bucketsful of hot water," he replied. "And a whirlpool bath in every bathroom." He looked down at her. "One of them holds two people."

She had mental images of being naked in it with Dawson, and her face paled. She withdrew from him without making a single move.

He tilted her chin up to his eyes. "I'm sorry. That could have been less crude."

She sighed. "It's early days yet," she said apologetically.

"Very early days." He pushed back her long, soft hair. "You let me kiss you," he added quietly. "Was it all an act, for her benefit?" He jerked his head toward the staircase.

"I don't act that well."

"Neither do I." His gaze fell to her mouth. "If we make haste slowly, we may discover that things fall into place."

"Things?"

He touched the very tip of her nose with his forefinger. "We might get rid of our scars."

She was worried, and looked it. "I don't know if I can—" she began uncertainly.

"That makes two of us," he said interrupting her.

She grimaced. "Sorry."

His chest rose and fell heavily. "One day at a time."

"Okay."

They took Leslie Holton riding that afternoon. She was surprisingly good on a horse, lithe and totally without fear. She seemed right at home on the ranch. If only she hadn't been making eyes at Dawson, Barrie could have enjoyed her company.

But Leslie Holton wanted Dawson, and she was working on ways to get him. The sudden engagement was very strange and she knew for a fact that Dawson had a reputation for avoiding women altogether. She thought Barrie was helping him put on an act, and if it took her every minute of her time here, she was going to unmask them. If Dawson really was cold, Leslie was going to find out why before she left.

Five

Unaware of Leslie Holton's plotting, Barrie was trying to concentrate on what Dawson was telling them about the history of the area they were riding through. But her eyes kept straying to the tall, proud way he rode, as if he were part of the horse. He looked good on horseback.

He looked good any way at all.

He caught her staring and smiled gently. Her heart skipped beats. He'd never been this way with her in all the time they'd known each other, and she couldn't believe he was faking it. There was a new tenderness in his eyes. He didn't talk to her in the old, mocking way. If she was different, so was he.

And through it all, there was an attraction that had its roots in the past. But Barrie was still afraid of intimacy with him. It was one thing to kiss him and hold hands with him. It was quite another to think of him in bed with her, demanding, insistent, totally out of control, hurting her . . . !

He glanced at her and saw that flash of fear, understood it without a word being spoken.

As Leslie rode ahead, he fell back beside Barrie. "Don't brood on it," he said seriously. "There's no rush. Give it time."

She sighed as she glanced toward him. "Reading my mind?"

"It isn't that difficult," he told her.

She toyed with the reins. "Time won't help," she said miserably. "I'm still afraid."

"My God, what is there to be afraid of?" he asked shortly. "Didn't you hear what I told you? I meant it. I can't, Barrie. I can't!"

She searched his eyes slowly. "You can't with other women," she corrected.

"I can't with you, either," he muttered. "Hell, don't you think I'd know after last night?"

She glanced warily ahead where Leslie was riding. "Last night you were holding back," she said.

"Yes, I was," he admitted. "You'd just had a nightmare and you were terrified. I didn't want to make it worse. But even this morning," he said heavily, averting his eyes to the horizon. His broad shoulders rose and fell. He couldn't bring himself to admit that even the hungry kiss he'd started to share with Barrie hadn't been able to arouse him.

Barrie noticed his reticence and kept her silence. She glanced around at the budding trees. Spring was her favorite season, although it certainly came later to Wyoming than it did to Arizona, even if May was basically the same in both places. Closer than the budding trees, however, was the irritated way Leslie Holton was glaring back at them.

"We aren't fooling her, you know," she said suddenly, and lifted her eyes to search his. "She thinks we're pretending."

"Aren't we?" he asked with a bitter laugh.

She supposed they were. Only it hadn't felt like pretense that morning on her part.

"That was a bald-faced lie," he murmured after a minute, and the saddle leather creaked as he reined in his horse and turned to look at her. His eyes were level and penetrating. "Suppose we try."

She felt her eyes widen. "Try...?"

"What you suggested last night. Or have you already forgotten where you put my hand?" he asked outrageously.

"Dawson!"

"You should look shocked. That was how I felt."

"That's right," she agreed, "pretend it was the first time a woman ever offered you any such thing!"

He managed a wistful smile. It had been a very long time since he'd been able to laugh about his body's lack of interest in women. "I can't," he admitted.

"That doesn't surprise me."

He drew up one long leg and wrapped it around the pommel, straining his powerful muscles against the thick fabric of his designer jeans. He leaned against it to study her, pigtailed and wearing similar clothing, jeans and a loose shirt. "You don't wear revealing clothes around me."

She shrugged. "No. Because I don't have to fight you off."

He cocked an eyebrow inquiringly.

She grimaced. "Well, men come on to me all the time, and I don't want any sort of physical relationship. So I flaunt my figure and flirt and talk about how much my family wants to see me get married and have a big family. You'd be amazed at how fast they find excuses to stop seeing me."

He chuckled. "Suppose someday a man calls your bluff?"

"That hasn't ever happened."

"Hasn't it?"

She realized what he meant, and her cheeks burned.

"I don't suppose I even bothered to tell you that I'd never seen a body more perfect," he continued quietly. "Barrie, undressed, you could pose for the Venus de Milo. I'm not sure that you wouldn't make her jealous."

She wasn't sure if it was a compliment or a dig, because their relationship had shifted in the past two days.

"I mean it," he explained, so that there wasn't any doubt. "And if I were still the man I was five years ago, you'd need a dead bolt on your door."

She searched his eyes. "I suppose at one time or another someone's ventured the opinion that your problem is mental and not physical?"

"Sure. I know that already. The thing is," he added with a faint smile, "how to cure it. And you seem to have a similar hang-up."

She shrugged. "From the same source."

"Yes, I know."

She traced around her pommel. "The obvious solution..."

He swung his leg back down and straightened as Leslie, missing them, came back to find them. "I'm not capable," he said shortly.

"I wasn't offering," she muttered. She glared toward Mrs. Holton. "Of course, she would, in a New York minute!"

He cocked an eyebrow. "Maybe I should let her try," he said cynically. "She probably knows tricks even I haven't learned."

"Dawson!"

He glanced at her, and he didn't smile. "Jealous?"

She moved restlessly in the saddle. "I...don't know. Maybe." She searched his face. "I wish I could offer you the same medicine she could. But you'd have to get me stinking drunk,'' she said on a pained laugh. She averted her eyes. ''I'd never forgive you if you did.''

''Did what? Get you stinking drunk?''

''No!'' she said at once. ''Do it ... with her,'' she explained.

His caught breath carried, but before he could reply, Leslie reined in beside them. ''Aren't you two coming along?'' she drawled. ''It's lonely trying to explore a ranch this size on my own.''

''Sorry,'' Dawson said, easing his horse into step beside hers. ''We were discussing plans.''

''I have a few of my own,'' Leslie murmured sweetly. ''Want to hear them?''

Barrie fell back a little, glaring at them. But Dawson wasn't having that. He stopped and motioned to her to catch up, with eyes that dared her to hesitate. Reluctantly she rode up beside him and kept pace, to Leslie's irritation, all the way home.

She'd thought Dawson would forget what she'd said before Leslie interrupted them. But he didn't. While Leslie was changing clothes before supper, Dawson caught Barrie by the hand and led her into his study that overlooked the cottonwood-lined river below.

He closed the door behind them and, as an afterthought, locked it.

She stood by the desk at the window, watching him warily. ''I gather that you wanted to talk to me?'' she asked defensively.

''Among other things.'' He perched himself on the edge of the desk facing her, and searched her wary face. He folded his arms across his broad chest. ''You kissed me back this morning,'' he said. ''You weren't doing it in case Leslie was watching, either. You've buried everything you used to feel for me, but it's still there. I want to try to dig it back up again.''

She studied her hands in her lap. It was tempting, because, despite everything that had happened, she loved Dawson. But the memories were too fresh even now, the pain too real. She couldn't block out the years of sarcastic remarks, cutting words, that had wounded her so badly.

She didn't know what he was offering, other than an attempt at a physical relationship. He'd said nothing about loving her. She knew he felt guilty about the baby she'd lost, and the knowledge of her miscarriage was very new to him. When he had time to cope with the grief, he might find that all he really felt for her was pity. She wanted much more than that.

She traced a chipped place on one neat fingernail.

"Well?" he asked impatiently.

She lifted her eyes. "I agreed to pretend to be engaged to you," she said quietly. "I don't want to live in Sheridan for the rest of my life, or give up the promotion I've been offered at my school in Tucson." He started to speak, but she held up her hand. "I know all too well how wealthy you are, Dawson, I know that I could have anything I wanted. But I'm used to making my own way in the world. I don't want to become your dependent."

"There are schools in Sheridan," he said shortly.

"Yes. There are good schools in Sheridan, and I'm sure I could get a position teaching in one. But they'd know my connection to you. I could never be sure if I got the job on my merit or yours."

He glared at her. This wasn't at all what he'd expected, especially after the way she'd softened toward him since last night.

"Don't you feel anything for me?" he asked.

She dropped her eyes to the emerald ring on her engagement finger. "I care for you, of course. I always will. But marriage is more than I can give you."

He got off the desk and turned away to the window. "You blame me for the baby, is that it?"

She glanced at his straight back. "I don't blame anyone. It wasn't preventable."

His head lifted a little higher. At his nape, his blond hair had grown slightly over his collar and it had a faint wave in it. Her eyes searched over his strong neck lovingly. She wanted nothing in life more than to live with him and love him. But what he was offering was a hollow relationship. Perhaps once he was over his guilt about the baby, he'd be able to function with a woman again. It was only a temporary problem, she was certain, caused by his unexpected discovery that she'd become pregnant and lost their child. But marriage wasn't the answer to the problem.

"We can have therapy," he said after a minute, grudgingly. "Perhaps they can find a cure for my impotence and your fear."

"I don't think your problem needs any therapy," she said. "It's just knowing about the baby that's caused it..."

He whirled, his eyes flashing. "I didn't know about the baby five years ago!" he said curtly.

She stared at him blankly for a minute, until she understood what he'd just said. Her face began to go pale. "Five years!" she stammered.

He glowered at her. "Didn't you realize what I was telling you?"

"I had no idea," she began. Her breath expelled sharply. "Five years!"

He looked embarrassed. He turned back to the window. He didn't speak.

She couldn't find any words to offer him. It hadn't occurred to her that a man could go for five years without sex. She eased out of her chair and went to the window to look up at him.

"I had no idea," she said again.

His hands were clasped behind him. His eyes were staring blankly at the flat horizon. "I haven't wanted anyone," he said. "When I found out about the baby, I was devastated. And yes, I felt guilty as well. One reason I asked you back here was to share the grief I felt, because I was pretty sure that you felt it, too, and had never really expressed it." He glanced down at her wistfully. "Maybe I hoped I could feel something with you, too. I wanted to be a whole man again, Barrie. But even that failed." His eyes went back to the window. "Stay until Leslie leaves. Help me keep what little pride I have left. Then I'll let you go."

She wasn't sure what to say to him. That he was devastated was obvious. So was she. Five years without a woman. She could hardly imagine the beating his ego had taken. It was impossible to offer comfort. She had her own feelings of inadequacy and broken pride.

"Everything would have been so different if we hadn't gone to France that summer," she said absently.

"Would it?" He turned to look at her. "Sooner or later, it would have happened, wherever we were. I know how my father felt," he added enigmatically.

"I'll stay until the widow leaves. But what about your land? She doesn't seem excited about selling."

"She will be, when I make her an offer. I happen to know that Powell Long is temporarily strapped for ready cash because of an expansion project on his ranch. He won't be able to match what I offer, and she's in a shaky financial situation. She can't afford to wait a long time for a buyer who'll offer more."

She was curious now. "Then if you know she'll sell, why am I here?"

"For the reason I told you in the beginning," he replied. His eyes were old and tired. "I can't let her find out that everything they've said about me is true. I do have a little pride left.''

She grimaced. ''It won't do any good if I tell you that...''

He touched his forefinger to her mouth. ''No. It won't do any good.''

She searched his eyes quietly. She felt inadequate. She felt sick all over. Somewhere in the back of her mind, she knew that the only hope he had of regaining a normal appetite was with her. The problem had begun in France. Only she would have the power to end it. But she didn't have the courage to try.

''Don't beat a dead horse,'' he said heavily, and managed a smile. ''I've learned to live with it. I'll get along. So will you. Go back to Tucson and take that job. You'll do them proud.''

''What will you do?'' she asked. ''There must be a way, someway...!''

''If there was, I'd have found it in five years' time,'' he said. He turned away from her and started toward the door. ''We'd better make an appearance.''

''Wait.''

He paused with his hand on the lock.

She ran her hands through her hair, drew a finger over her mouth, opened the top button of her blouse and drew part of the shirttail out.

He understood what she was doing. He pulled out his handkerchief and gave it to her. She drew it lightly over the corner of her mouth and handed it back.

Then he unlocked the door, to find Leslie sitting on the bottom step of the staircase. She eyed them suspiciously and when she saw Barrie's attempts at reparation, she made an impatient sound.

''Sorry,'' Dawson murmured. ''We forgot the time.''

''Obviously,'' Leslie said shortly, glaring at Barrie. ''I did come here to talk about land.''

"So you did. I'm at your disposal," Dawson said. "Would you like to talk over a cup of coffee?"

"No, I'd like to drive into town with you and see some of the sights," she said. She glanced at Barrie. "I suppose she'll have to come, too."

"Not if you'd rather have my undivided attention," Dawson said surprisingly. "You don't mind, do you, honey?" he added.

Barrie was unsettled, but she forced a smile to her tight lips. "Of course not. Go right ahead. I'll help Corlie bake a cake."

"Can you cook?" Leslie asked indifferently. "I never bothered to learn how. I eat out most of the time."

"I hate restaurant food and fast food," Barrie remarked, "so I took a culinary course last summer. I can even do French pastries."

Dawson was watching her. "You never mentioned that."

She shrugged. "You never asked," she said coolly.

"How odd," Leslie interjected. "I thought engaged people knew all about each other. And she *is* your stepsister," she added.

"We've spent some time apart," he explained. "We're still in the learning stages, despite the engagement. We won't be long," he told Barrie.

"Take your time."

He hesitated, and Barrie knew why. She didn't want to give Leslie any excuse to taunt him. She went forward, sliding her arms around his waist and trying not to notice how he stiffened.

"Remember that you're engaged," she said in a stage whisper, and went on tiptoe to put her lips to his.

They were as cold as ice, like the eyes that never closed, even though he gave the appearance of returning her caress.

"We'll expect something special on the table when we get back," he said, and gently put her away from him.

Barrie felt empty somehow. She knew he wasn't capable of giving her a full response, but she'd hoped for more warmth than he'd shown her. He looked at her as if he hated her. Perhaps he still did.

Her sad eyes made him uncomfortable. He took Leslie's arm with a smile and led her out the door toward the garage behind the house.

"Trouble in your engagement already?" Leslie mused as they drove out of town in Dawson's new silver Mercedes. "I notice that you're suddenly very cool toward your fiancée. Of course, there is a rather large age difference between you, isn't there?"

Dawson only shrugged. "Every engagement has a few rough spots that need smoothing over," he said carelessly.

"This one was sudden."

"Not on my part," he replied as he slowed to make a turn.

"I begin to understand. Unrequited love?"

He laughed bitterly. "It seemed that way for a few years."

Leslie stared at him curiously, and then all at once she began laughing.

His eyebrows lifted in a silent query.

"I'm sorry." She choked through her laughter. "It's just that there were these rumors going around about you," she confessed. "I don't know why I even believed them."

"Rumors?" he asked, deadpan.

"Oh, they're too silly to repeat. And now they make sense. I suppose you simply gave up dating women you didn't care about."

He hadn't expected that Leslie might be so easy to placate about those rumors. He glanced at her, scowling.

She only smiled, and this time without overt flirting. "It's kind of sweet, really," she mused. "Barrie didn't suspect?"

He averted his eyes. "No."

"She still doesn't suspect, does she?" she asked curiously. "You're engaged, but she acts as if it's difficult for her even to kiss you. And don't think I was fooled by that very obvious lipstick smear on your handkerchief," she added with a grin. "There wasn't a trace of it on your face, or a red mark where you might have wiped it off. She's very nervous with you, and it shows."

He knew that, but he didn't like hearing it. "It's early days yet."

She nodded slowly. "You might consider that she has less experience with men than she pretends," she added helpfully. "She hasn't got that faint edge of sophistication most women of her age have acquired. I don't think she's very worldly at all."

He pulled the car into a parking spot in front of the old county courthouse. "You see a lot for someone who pretends to have a hard edge of her own," he said flatly, pinning her with his pale green eyes.

She leaned back in her comfortable seat. "I was in love with my husband," she said unexpectedly. "Everybody thought I married him for his money, because he was so much older than I was. It wasn't true. I married him because he was the first person in my life who was ever kind to me." Her voice became bitter with memories. "My father had no use for me, because he never believed I was his child. My mother hated me because I had to be taken care of, and she wanted to party. In the end, they both left me to my own devices. I fell in with bad company and got in trouble with the law." Her thin shoulders lifted and fell. "I was sentenced to a year in prison for helping my latest boyfriend steal some cigarettes. Jack Holton was in court at the time representing a client on some misdemeanor and he started talking to me during the recess." She smiled, remembering. "I was a hard case, but he was interested and very persistent. I was married before I knew it." She stared at her skirt, distracted by memories. "When he died, I went a little mad. I don't think I came to my senses until today." She looked up. "Barrie has something in her past, something that's hurt her. Go easy, won't you?"

He was surprised by her perception. But it was beyond him to admit to a relative stranger how Barrie had been hurt, and by whom. "I'll keep it in mind," he replied.

She smiled at him with genuine fondness. "I do like you, you know," she said. "You're a lot like Jack. But now that I know how things stand, you're off the endangered list. Now how much do you want to offer me for that tract of land?"

He chuckled. He hadn't expected it to be this easy, but he wasn't looking a gift horse in the mouth.

When he came back with Leslie, his arm around her shoulder and all smiles, Barrie was immediately on the defensive. She had all sorts of ideas about why they were both smiling and so relaxed with each other. She was furiously jealous and hurt, and she didn't know how to cope with her own reactions.

She was silent at the dinner table, withdrawn and introspective, speaking only when addressed. It was the first glimmer of hope that she'd given a pensive Dawson. If she could still feel jealous about him, there was hope that he hadn't killed all her feelings for him.

So he laid it on with Leslie.

"I think we ought to have a celebration party," he announced. "Friday night. We'll phone out invitations and have a dance. Corlie will love making the arrangements."

"Can she do it, on such short notice?" Leslie asked.

"Of course! Barrie will help, too, won't you?" he added with a smile in his fiancée's direction.

"Certainly," Barrie replied in a lackluster voice.

"I have some wonderful CDs, just perfect for dancing to," Leslie added. "Including some old forties torch songs," she added flirtatiously. "Do you dance, Barrie?" she asked.

"I haven't in quite some time," the other woman replied politely. "But I suppose it's like riding a bicycle, isn't it?"

"It will come back to you," Dawson assured her. His eyes narrowed as he stared at her. "If you've forgotten the steps, I'm sure I can teach you."

She glanced up, flushing a little as she met his calculating stare. "I'm learning all the time," she said shortly.

He lifted an eyebrow and grinned at Leslie. "We'll have a good time," he promised her. "And now, suppose we go over that contract I had my attorney draw up, just to make sure it's in order? Barrie, you won't mind, will you?" he added.

Barrie lifted her chin proudly. "Certainly not," she replied. "After all, it's just business, isn't it?"

"What else would it be?" he drawled.

What else indeed! Barrie thought furiously as she watched him close the study door behind himself and the widow Holton.

She went up to her room and locked the door. She'd never been so furious in all her life. He'd wanted her to come here and pretend to be engaged to him to keep the widow at bay, and now he was behaving as if it were the widow he was engaged to! Well, he needn't expect her to stay and be a doormat! He could have his party Friday, and she'd be on her way out of town first thing Saturday morning. If he liked the widow, he could have her.

She lay down on the bed and tears filled her eyes. Who was she kidding? She still loved him. It was just like old times. Dawson knew how she felt and he was putting the knife into her heart again. What an idiot she'd been to believe anything he told her. He was probably laughing his head off at how easily he'd tricked her into coming here, so that he could taunt her some more. Apparently she was still being made to pay for his father's second marriage. And she'd hoped that he was learning to care for her. Ha! She might as well cut her losses. She'd tell him tomorrow, she decided. First thing.

Six

___

Barrie told Dawson that she'd be leaving after the party. Her statement was met with an icy silence and a glare that would have felled a lesser woman.

"We're engaged," he said flatly.

"Are we?" She took off the emerald ring and laid it on his desk. "Try it on the widow's finger. Maybe it will fit her."

"You don't understand," he said through his teeth. "She's only selling me the tract. There's nothing to be jealous of."

Her eyebrows lifted. "Jealous?" she drawled sarcastically. "Why, Dawson, why should I be jealous? After all, I've got half a football team of men just panting to take me out back in Tucson."

He hadn't had a comeback. The remark threw him completely off-balance. By the time he regained it, cursing his own lack of foresight, she'd gone out the door.

And until the night of the party, she kept him completely at bay with plastic smiles and polite conversation.

It had been a long Friday evening, and all Barrie wanted was to go back to her room and get away from Dawson. All night she'd watched women, mostly Leslie Holton, fawn over him while he smiled that cynical smile and ate up the attention. He wasn't backing away from Leslie tonight. Odd, that sudden change.

Barrie had been studiously avoiding both of them all night, so much so that Corlie, helping serve canapés and drinks, was scowling ominously at her. But Barrie couldn't help her coldness toward Dawson. She felt as if he'd sold her out all over again.

The surprise came when Leslie Holton announced that she was going to leave and went to her car instead of her room. Barrie watched from the doorway as Leslie reached up and kissed Dawson deliberately. And he didn't pull away, either. It was the last straw. She went back inside with bottled fury. Damn him!

He came back inside just as Barrie was saying goodbye to the last of their few guests. She tried to ease out, but while he said good-night to the departing guest, Dawson's arm came across the doorway and blocked her exit. He seemed to know that she'd withdraw instinctively from his touch, because he smiled without humor when she stepped back.

The visitor left. Dawson closed the door with a snap and turned to her, his narrow green eyes cold and calculating.

"Why?" she asked and tried not to sound afraid.

His eyes ran the length of her, from her loosened wavy dark hair to her trim figure and long, elegant legs in the short black dress.

"Maybe I'm tired of playing games," he said enigmatically.

"With me or Leslie Holton?" she demanded.

"You don't know why I played up to Leslie?" he drawled. "You can't guess?"

Her face colored delicately. "I don't want to know why. I want to go to bed, Dawson," she said, measuring the distance to the door.

He let out a long, weary sigh and moved closer, noticing with resignation her rigid posture and the fear that came into her eyes.

"You run. I run. What the hell difference has it made?" he asked. His hands shot out and caught her shoulders. He pulled her to him, ignoring her struggles, and held her against the lean warmth of his powerful body. "If I ruined your young life, you damn sure ruined mine," he said under his breath, staring at her mouth. "I thought we were getting closer and now we're worlds apart, all over again. Come here.

Two neat whiskies had loosened all his inhibitions. He dragged her to him without caring that he couldn't feel anything physically. He could kiss her, at least . . .

And he did, with aching need, his mind yielded to the feel and touch and taste of her. He groaned as he drew her even closer, feeling her go rigid against him as his mouth parted her soft lips. But her resistance didn't stop him. He gave in to his hunger without any thought except to show her that he couldn't be aroused by even the most ardent kiss.

But what he expected to happen, didn't. He drew her hips to his and the sudden touch of her long legs against his made him shudder and all at once, his body exploded with hunger, need, anguished desire. His intake of breath was audible, shocking as he felt a full, raging arousal for the first time in almost five years.

He dragged his mouth from hers and looked down at her with horror and dawning realization. The curse he spat out shocked even Barrie, who'd heard them all at one time or another from very modern grammar school students. His face looked frightening and his hands tightened until they hurt.

She reacted purely with instinct, fighting the pain he was unknowingly inflicting. She struggled away from him, breathing roughly, rubbing the arms he'd held in that steely grip.

He wasn't even aware of having hurt her. He just stood there, glaring at her, shivering with the force of his desire for her. He wanted her with pure obsession and she couldn't bear him to touch her. It was ironic. Tragic. He'd only just discovered that he was still capable with one woman at least, and she had to be the one woman on earth who couldn't bear him to touch her.

He stared at her with narrow, bitter eyes. "God, that was all it needed!" he said in anguish, his face tormented as he met her eyes. "That was damn all!"

He was looking at her as if he hated her, with wild eyes, while she stood gaping at him. He'd said he couldn't feel anything! She didn't realize that she'd said it aloud.

He ran a rough hand through his wavy blond hair and drew it over his brow as he turned away. "I thought I was dead from the waist down, that I was immune to any woman. I never realized why, even if I suspected it . . . I might as well be dead!" he said huskily. "My God, I might as well be!"

He threw open the door and went out it as if he'd forgotten Barrie's presence altogether, reaching his car in long, angry strides. He jerked the door open, started it, and took off.

Barrie watched him as if she were a sleepwalker until it suddenly dawned on her that he was acting totally unlike himself. She'd seen him down two neat whiskies, but would that have been enough to make him lose control so completely?

"Dawson," she said to herself, because he was already out of sight.

She stood helplessly in the doorway, trying to decide what to do. He was in no condition to be driving. How could she go to bed now? On the other hand, how could she stay down here? He might be even more violent when he returned. She remembered, oh, too well, what Dawson was like when he was out of control. Corlie and Rodge had gone to bed. She couldn't bear the thought of being alone with him . . . But the way he'd driven off had been frightening too. What if he hurt himself?

With a concern that grew by the minute, she rushed to get her wrap and purse and the keys to Dawson's MG that hung by the back door. She'd drive down the road, she thought, just to make sure he hadn't run into a ditch or something. That would make her feel better. And if she didn't see him, she could assume that he was all right and go back to her room. Not that it was going to make her stop worrying. She'd never seen him so shaken, so wild. Dawson never lost control. Well, only that once. But even that hadn't been such a total loss of reason. The alcohol would have made it worse, too.

Her mind made up, she started off in the general direction Dawson had taken. The headlights of the sports car picked up nothing on the side of the road for at least two miles down the deserted highway, and she breathed a sigh of relief. He was probably on his way back to the house even . . .

Her heart jumped when she saw the flashing lights over the next rise. She knew, somewhere deep inside her, that Dawson was where they were. She stepped on the accelerator and began to pray as a cold sickness grew in the pit of her stomach.

It could have been worse, but not much. The car had overturned. She caught sight of skid marks on the black pavement, and the sheriff's deputy patrol car on the side of the road. Even as she pulled off the road and stopped, she could hear an ambulance in the distance.

She threw the MG out of gear and left it idling and ran frantically to the median where Dawson's Jaguar lay crushed with its wheels in the air.

"Dawson!" she screamed. Her heart was beating so fast that she shook with it. "Oh, God!"

The sheriff's deputy stopped her headlong flight.

"Let me go." She wept piteously, fighting him. "Please, please . . . !"

"You can't help him like this," he said firmly. "You recognize the car?"

"It's Dawson," she whispered. "Dawson Rutherford. My stepbrother . . . is he . . . dead?"

It seemed forever before he answered. "Not yet," he said. "Calm down."

She looked up at him in the glare of the flashing lights. "Please!" she whispered, reduced to begging as she tugged against his firm hold. "Oh, God, please, please . . . !"

The officer was basically a kind man, and that look would have touched a career criminal. With a rough sigh, he let go of her.

Heart pounding savagely, eyes wide with fear, she ran headlong to the car, where Dawson lay in a curious position in the wreckage. Blood was coming from somewhere. When she touched his jacket, she felt it on her hands. She knew not to try to move him. His face was turned away. She touched his hair with trembling hands. It was icy cold, like the skin on his face. Her hands cradled what she could reach of him, as if by touching and holding, she could keep him alive.

"You mustn't . . . die," she whispered brokenly. "Dawson, please! Oh, God, please, Dawson, you mustn't die!"

There was no movement at all, no answer. He seemed to be pinned. She couldn't tell where in the darkness. Behind her, the ambulance siren came closer. She heard it stop, heard voices. Another vehicle pulled up, too.

Gentle, but firm hands moved her away, back into the care of the deputy. This time she stood silently, unmoving, watching, waiting. She'd thought so many times that she hated Dawson, especially since he'd played up to Leslie, but she'd only been lying to herself. She might have legions of dates, men who wanted her, but there was only one man that she loved. Despite the pain and anguish of the past, her heart was lying in that tangled wreckage. And she knew then, for certain, that if Dawson died, part of her would die with him. She only wished that she'd had time to tell him so.

They had to cut him out of the Jaguar. When they put him on the stretcher, he didn't move. His face was almost white. They covered him with a blanket and carried him to the waiting ambulance. Barrie stared at him, at the ambulance, with dull, dead eyes. Was he gone? He didn't move. Perhaps he was already dead and they didn't want to cover him up in front of her. But her heart was still beating. She was still breathing. Surely if he was dead, she would be, too.

"Come on," the deputy said gently. "I'll drive you to the hospital."

"The . . . car," she faltered numbly.

"I'll take care of it." With the ease of years of practice, he attended to the car, loaded her into the patrol car and followed the ambulance back to the private hospital in Sheridan.

Barrie drank five cups of coffee before anyone came to tell him how he was. She didn't think at all. She sat staring out the window into the darkness, praying.

"Miss Rutherford?"

She looked up. "Bell," she corrected dully. "Dawson is my stepbrother." Her eyes pleaded for miracles.

And the doctor had one. He smiled wearily, his green mask dangling from his neck, lying on his stained surgical uniform. Blood, she noticed idly. Dawson's blood.

"He'll make it," he told her abruptly. "He was unconscious when they brought him in, probably due to the concussion he's sustained. But, miraculously, there was no internal damage. He didn't even break any bones, isn't that . . . Miss Bell!"

She came to lying on a bed in the emergency room. She saw the lights overhead and the whiteness of the ceiling. Dawson was going to live. The doctor had said so. Or had she dreamed it?

She turned her head, and a nurse smiled at her.

"Feeling better?" she asked. "You've had quite a night, I gather. Mr. Rutherford is in a private room, and he's doing fine. He came around a little while ago and asked about you."

Her heart jumped. "He was conscious?"

"Oh, very," she replied dryly. "We assured him that you were in the waiting room and he didn't say another word. He's going to be all right."

"Thank God," she breathed, closing her eyes again. "Oh, thank God."

"You must be very close," the nurse remarked.

Barrie could have laughed. "We don't have family," she said evasively. "Only each other."

"I see. Well, what a lucky thing that he was wearing his seat belt. He's very handsome," she added, and Barrie looked again, noticing the nurse's pretty blond hair and brown eyes.

"Yes, he is, isn't he?" Barrie replied.

The nurse finished working on her chart. "He's on my ward. Lucky me." She grinned.

Yes. Lucky you, Barrie thought, but she didn't say anything. She got up, with the nurse's help, and went to the rest room to freshen up. She tried not to think on the way. She'd had enough for one night.

After she'd bathed her face and retouched her makeup and combed her hair, she went along to Dawson's room. She peered around the door cautiously, but he was in a private room and alone. He was conscious, as the nurse had said.

His head turned as he heard her step and she grimaced at the cuts on one side of his handsome face. There was a bruise on his cheek and at his temple. He seemed a little disoriented, and it wasn't surprising, considering the condition the Jaguar had been in. She shuddered, remembering how he'd looked then.

His eyes narrowed. He breathed slowly, watching her approach. "Sorry," he managed to say in a hoarse tone.

She winced and tears overflowed her eyes. "You idiot!" she raged, sobbing. "You crazy idiot, you could have been killed!"

"Barrie," he said softly, holding out a hand.

She ran to him. The walls were well and truly down, as if they'd never existed. She all but fell into the chair beside the bed and lay across him, careless of the IV they were giving him, shivering as she felt his hands on her shoulders, holding her while she wept.

"Here, now," he chided weakly. "I'm all right. Lucky I hit my head and not some more vital part."

She didn't answer. Her body shook with sobs. She clung. She felt his hand in her hair, smoothing it, soothing her.

"Damn," he breathed roughly. "I'm so weak, Barrie."

"Weak is better than dead," she muttered as she finally lifted her head. Her red, swollen eyes met his.

"You're going to have a dandy bruise," she told him, sniffing, dabbing with her fingers at her wet cheeks and eyes.

"No doubt." He moved and winced. "God, what a headache. I don't know if it's the whiskey or the wreck." He frowned. "Why was I driving?" he added, struggling to regain complete control of his faculties after the concussion.

Her heart jumped. "I don't know, exactly," she said evasively. "You...got angry and stormed out to the car."

He whistled softly through pursed lips and smiled half-humorously. "Nice epitaph—dead for unknown reasons."

"Don't," she said, dabbing at her eyes with a tissue from the box by his bed. "It isn't funny."

"Were we arguing again?" he asked.

She shook her head. "Not really."

He frowned. "Then what...?"

The door opened again, and the pretty blond nurse danced in with a clipboard. "Time for vital signs again," she informed them. "This will only take a minute." She glanced at Barrie. "If you'd like to get a cup of coffee...?"

She didn't have the heart for an argument. "I'll be back soon," she said.

Dawson looked as if he wanted to say something, but the nurse popped her electronic thermometer in his mouth and he grimaced.

Later, Barrie went back to the house and phoned Antonia to tell her what was going on. She'd called Corlie and Rodge the night before, and they were waiting for her when she arrived. She took time to fill them in on Dawson's condition before she phoned her best friend in Bighorn.

"Do you want me to come over and sit with you?" Antonia asked.

"No," Barrie said. "I just needed someone to talk to. He'll be in for another day or so. I didn't want you to worry in case you tried to get in touch with me and wondered where I was. Especially after I'd told you I'd be back in Tucson today."

"Can we do anything?"

Barrie laughed. "No, but thanks. I'll keep you in mind. He's getting plenty of attention right now from a very pretty young nurse. I don't think he'll even miss me when I go."

There was a pause. "You aren't going to leave before they release him?"

"No," Barrie said reluctantly.

"You don't know why he was driving so recklessly?"

"Yes, I think I do," she said miserably. "It was partly my fault. But he'd had too much to drink, too. And he's the one who's always lecturing people about not driving under the influence."

"We can blackmail him for years on this," Antonia replied with a smile in her voice. "Thank God he'll be alive so that we can."

"I'll tell him you said so. If I can get his attention."

She hung up and went into the study, because she felt closer to Dawson there. She hadn't told him the truth about last night. She had a suspicion about why he'd gone out. He'd said it himself. He was only capable with one woman . . . the one woman he'd scarred too much to ever want sex again. And he couldn't bear the thought of it. How horribly ironic.

It did make sense, somehow. She went to the window to look out. The sky was gray and low with dark clouds. It was going to snow. She needed to get out before the roads became impassible, but she couldn't leave Dawson. What was she going to do? The first thing was to go back to the hospital.

But Corlie refused to let her. "You need food and rest. You've been up all night. Rodge and I will sit with him until you have a little rest."

"You don't have to do that," she began.

"Barrie, you know better than that. He's like our own child, mine and Rodge's. You eat something and we'll stay until you get back to be with him tonight."

"Okay."

Corlie seemed to take it for granted that Barrie was going to stay the night with him. Of course. Everyone still thought they were engaged. She grimaced. Dawson wasn't going to like that one bit. When he was back to himself he was going to hate her all over again. She was his one and only big mistake. He'd been furious at her when he'd stormed out. He seemed to actually hate her because he was aroused by her.

But he was subtly different. When she arrived back at the hospital, he watched her come in with eyes that were alert and searching.

"Feel better?" he asked quietly.

"That's my line," she murmured, smiling at Corlie and Rodge.

Corlie got up and hugged her warmly. "Honey, you're freezing," she chided. "Don't you have something heavier than that windbreaker to wear?"

"It doesn't exactly freeze in Tucson," Barrie reminded her.

"Go to Harper's and buy a coat," Dawson said. "I've got an account there."

"I don't need a coat," she said on a nervous laugh. "And I won't be here long enough to use it. Anyway, it's just a little nip in the air. It's spring."

He didn't reply. His eyes were watchful, curious. "Corlie, you know what size to buy?"

"Yes," Corlie said, grinning.

"Get her one."

"I'll do it first thing tomorrow."

"But . . . !" Barrie began.

"Hush, child. He's right, you'll freeze in that thing you're wearing. We'll be back early in the morning." She hugged Barrie again.

"Might as well not argue," Rodge said with a grin. "I haven't won an argument with her in thirty-five years. What chance would you have?"

"Not much," Barrie sighed.

They said their goodbyes to Dawson and went out the door, waving.

Barrie edged toward the chair beside the bed, feeling vulnerable now that they were alone. He was much too alert to suit her.

He watched her sit down, his eyes following her. He caught her gaze and held it relentlessly until she flushed and looked away.

"I've remembered," he said.

She bit her lower lip. "Have you?"

"And apparently you've realized why I lost my temper."

The flush got worse. She looked at the floor.

He laughed bitterly. "That's right, Barrie, try to pretend it didn't happen. Run some more." His hand shot out and caught her arm. "Stop that," he said curtly. "Your lip's bleeding."

She hadn't even felt the pain. She pulled out a tissue and held it to her lip. It came away red. "It's a habit," she faltered.

He let go of her arm and sank back against the pillows. He looked older. There were new lines in his face, around his eyes. He looked as if he'd never smiled once in his life.

She clutched the tissue in her hand. "Dawson?"

His gaze came back to hers, questioning.

"Why is it that you weren't...cold...with me?" she asked hesitantly. "I mean, all those other women, like Mrs. Holton...and she's a knockout."

He searched her eyes. "I don't know why, Barrie," he replied. "Maybe it's because I hurt you so badly. Maybe it's what hell really is. I want you and you're physically afraid of me. Ironic, isn't it? Do you have any idea, any idea at all, how it makes a man feel to know that he's impotent?"

She shook her head. "Not really."

"All these long years," he said, brushing the unruly hair back from his broad forehead. His eyes closed. "It makes me sick when women touch me, fawn over me. I don't feel anything, Barrie. It seemed to be like that with you. That's why I pulled you against me that way, I wanted to show you what you'd done to me." He laughed with bitter irony. "And I got the lesson, didn't I? It was the most violent, raging arousal I've ever had in my life— with the one woman who shudders at my touch." His eyes closed.

She clenched her teeth as she studied him. She'd loved him all her life, it sometimes seemed. And then in one short night, he'd destroyed her love, her future, her femininity. If his life was hopeless, so was hers.

He glanced at her. "It's been that bad for you, too, hasn't it?" he asked suddenly, with narrowed eyes that seemed to see right through her. "All those damn men parading through your life in a constant, steady stream, in threes and fours. And you've never let one of them touch you, not even in the most innocent way."

She shivered. It was too much. It was too much, having him know that about her. He might as well have stripped her soul naked.

She started to jump up, but he caught her wrist with surprising strength for a man in his condition and jerked her firmly right back down into the chair again.

"No," he said, glaring at her. "No, you don't. You aren't running this time. I said, you've never let anyone touch you, in any way, even to kiss you, since me. Go ahead. Tell me I'm lying."

She swallowed. Her face gave him the answer.

His lips parted. He exhaled softly. "Damn me, Barrie," he said huskily. "Damn me for that."

He let go of her wrist and lay back on the bed. "For the first time in my life, I don't know what to do," he confessed dully.

He sounded defeated. Dawson, of all people. She hated that uncertainty in his deep voice. She hated what they'd done to each other. He was her whole world.

She reached out, very slowly. Her cold fingers just barely touched his bare arm, just at the elbow.

As if he couldn't believe what his senses were telling him, he turned his head and looked at her pale hand on his arm. His eyes lifted to hers, curious, intent.

She bit her lip again. "I don't want you to die," she said unsteadily.

He looked at her fingers, curled hesitantly around his arm. "Barrie..."

Before he could get the words out, the door opened and the pretty nurse was back again, smiling, cheerful, full of optimism and already possessive about her handsome patient.

"Supper," she announced, putting a tray on the table. "Soup and tea, and I'm going to feed you myself!"

"Like hell you are," Dawson said curtly.

The nurse started. His eyes weren't welcoming at all. They had a very cobralike quality, flashing warnings at her. She laughed with a sudden loss of confidence and pushed the high, wheeled tray over to the bed. "Well, of course, if you feel like feeding yourself, you can." She cleared her throat. "I'll be back to pick it up in a few minutes. Try to eat it all, now."

She smiled again, but with less enthusiasm, and went out the door much more quickly than she'd come in.

Dawson took a pained breath. His head turned toward Barrie. "Help me," he said quietly.

It was intimate, helping him eat. She watched every mouthful disappear past those thin, firm lips, and without wanting to, she remembered the feel of them on her mouth in passion. She'd been innocent and very frightened. He hadn't realized that. His kisses had been adult, passionate, giving no quarter. She knew that he'd never even suspected that she was a total innocent until...

Her flush was revealing. Dawson swallowed the last of the soup and caught her gaze.

"I have my own nightmares," he said unexpectedly. "If I could take it back, I would. Believe that, at least."

She moved restlessly as she put the soup bowl back on the table and helped him sip some of the hot tea. He made a terrible face.

"It's good for you," she said stubbornly.

"It may be good as a hand warmer in a cup on a cold day," he muttered. "If it's good for anything else, I wouldn't know." He lay back down. "If they want to shovel caffeine in me, why can't I have coffee?"

"Ask someone who knows."

He chuckled without humor. His eyes searched hers. "Going to stay with me tonight?"

"It seems to be expected."

His face hardened. "Don't let me put you out. I'm perfectly capable..."

She winced.

He closed his eyes. Beside his thigh, his fist clenched until the knuckles went white.

She pulled her chair closer. Her fingers spread tremulously over his big fist and lingered there. "Dawson, don't," she whispered. "Of course I'll stay. I want to."

He didn't say a word. And still, his hand clenched.

Her fingers pressed down, became caressing.

She knew when his head turned, when his eyes opened. She knew that he was watching her. With a long, helpless sigh, she lifted his hand and put it to her lips. And he shuddered.

She dropped it abruptly, horrified at her own action, and started to get up, red-faced.

But he had her hand now, turned in his, firmly held. He drew it until he could press the palm to his hard mouth. His eyes closed and he made a sound deep in his throat. When he looked at her again, what she saw in his face made her go hot all over.

"Come here," he said huskily.

Her knees became weak. She felt the imprint of his mouth on her palm as if it were a brand. She never knew whether or not she would have obeyed that heated command, though, because the door opened and the doctor, making rounds, came in smiling. Dawson let go of her hand and the moment was lost.

But not forgotten. Not at all, not through the long night when he slept, because of the pills they gave him, and she lay in the chair and watched him sleep. They seemed to have reached some sort of turning point. Her life lay in that hospital bed now. She had no desire whatsoever to leave him. And it seemed to be the same for him.

When he woke the next morning, a new young nurse came in with soap and a towel and a basin of water. Her eyes were bright and flirting, but when she offered to bathe him, he gave her a look that made her excuse herself and leave.

"You're intimidating the nurses," Barrie remarked with a faint smile. She was tired and half-asleep, but the look he'd given the nurse amused her.

"I don't want them touching me."

"You're not up to bathing yourself," she protested.

His eyes searched hers without amusement, without taunting. "Then you do it," he said quietly. "Because yours are the only hands I want on my body."

She stared at him helplessly. He wasn't chiding her now. His eyes were warm and quiet and soft on her face.

She got up, a little hesitant. "I've never bathed anyone except myself," she said.

He untied the hospital gown at the neck and, holding her eyes, sloughed it off, leaving the sheet over his lean hips.

She colored a little. She'd never seen him undressed, despite their intimacy.

"It's all right," he said, soothing her. "I'll leave the cover where it is. I can do the rest myself, when you finish."

She didn't stop to ask why he couldn't do it all. Her hands went to the cloth. She wet it, and put soap on it. Then, with gentle motions, she drew it over his face and throat and back, rinsing it and him before she put more soap on the cloth again and hesitated at his arms and chest.

"I'm not in a place, or in a position, to cause you any worry," he said gently.

She managed a smile. She drew the cloth down his arms, to his lean, strong hands, and back up to his collarbone. She rinsed it again before she began to smooth it, slowly over the thick hair on his chest. Even through the cloth, she could feel the warm muscles, the thickness of the hair. She remembered just for an instant the feel and smell and taste of his chest under her lips, when she'd been all but fainting with desire for him.

He felt her hesitate. His hand pressed down on hers. "It's only flesh and bone," he said quietly. "Nothing to be afraid of."

She nodded. Her hand smoothed down to his navel, his flat stomach. He groaned suddenly and caught her fingers, staying them.

His breath came erratically. He laughed abruptly. "I think...you'd better stop there."

Her hand stilled. Involuntarily her eyes slipped past it, and she stared.

"One of the pitfalls of bathing a man," he said, swallowing hard. "Although I won't pretend not to enjoy it. For years, that hasn't happened at all."

Her eyes were curious as they met his.

"You don't understand," he mused.

She smiled faintly. "Not really."

"That doesn't happen with other women," he explained slowly. "Not at all."

"And if it doesn't, you can't—" She stopped.

He nodded. "Exactly."

Evading his intent gaze, she lifted the cloth and rinsed it and then soaped it again. She handed it to him. "Here. You'd better..."

His hand touched hers. He searched her eyes. "Please," he whispered.

She bit her lip. "I can't!"

"Why?" He didn't even blink. "Is it repulsive, to touch me like that, to look at me?"

Her face was a flaming red. "I've never... looked!"

"Don't you want to?" he asked gently. "Honestly?"

She didn't speak. She didn't move, either. His hand went to the sheet and he pulled it away slowly, folding it back on his powerful thighs.

"We made love once," he said quietly. "You were part of me. I'm not embarrassed to let you look. And I'll tell you for a fact, I'd never let another woman see me helpless like this." He took a long, slow breath and felt the tension drain out of him. He was weak and disoriented, and his body relaxed completely. It worried him a little that he couldn't maintain the tension, but when he was well again, perhaps he could find out if he really was capable completely. Unaware of his misgivings, Barrie bit down hard on her lip, and let her eyes slide down. She looked and then couldn't look away. He was...beautifully made. He was like one of the nude statues she'd seen in art books. But he was real.

She tried to use the cloth, but it was just too much too soon. With a smile and a grimace she finally gave in to her shyness and turned away while he finished the chore.

"Don't feel bad," he said gently when he was covered again, and the bath things were put aside. "It's a big step for both of us, I guess. These things take time."

She nodded.

He tugged her down into the chair beside the bed. "Do you realize that we made love and never saw each other undressed?"

"You shouldn't talk about it," she faltered.

"You were innocent and I was a fool," he said. "I rushed at you like a bull in heat, and I never even realized how innocent you were until I hurt you. And I couldn't accept that you were, Barrie," he confessed heavily. "Because if I admitted that, I had to accept what I'd done to you, how I'd scarred you. Maybe my body was more honest than I was. It didn't want another woman after you. It still doesn't. The reaction you get, I can't give to anyone else."

She met his eyes. "I don't...want anyone else, either," she said softly.

"Do you want me?" he asked bluntly. "Are you able to want me?"

She smiled sadly. "I don't know, Dawson."

He took her hand and held it tight. "Maybe that's something that we're both going to have to find out, when I leave here," he said, and it sounded as if he dreaded the outcome as much as she did.

Seven

They let Dawson go home three days after he was admitted. The doctor insisted that he be cautious about returning to work, and that if he had any recurring symptoms from the head injury, he was to get in touch. Barrie wasn't happy about them discharging him, but she did have every sympathy with the nursing staff. Dawson in a recovered state was better off without time on his hands. He made everyone uncomfortable.

He'd progressed from the bed to the desk in his study and he'd taken Barrie in there with him to discuss the tract of land Leslie Holton had agreed to sell him.

She stared at the contract on the desk, which had arrived by special courier that morning. "She wasn't that eager to sell at first. How did you change her mind?" she asked with barely contained irritation.

He leaned back in his chair, his forehead still purplish from its impact with the steering wheel, marred by the thin line of stitches that puckered the tanned flesh.

"How do you think I convinced her?" he taunted.

She didn't say a word. But her face spoke silently.

He smiled cynically. "And that's a false conclusion if I ever saw one," he mused. "I can't do that with anyone except you, Barrie."

She flushed a little. "You don't know that."

"Don't I?" His pale eyes slid down her body which was in a loose knit shirt and jeans, and lingered on the thrust of her high breasts. "Then let's say that I'm not interested in finding out if I can want anyone else."

"You'd been drinking," she reminded him.

"So I had." He stood up. "And you think it was the whiskey?"

She shrugged. "It might have been."

He moved away from the desk, glanced at her thoughtfully for a moment, and then on an impulse, went to close and lock the office door. "Let's see," he murmured deeply, and moved toward her.

She jumped behind a wing chair and gripped it for dear life. Her eyes were wide, wild. "No!"

He paused, searching her white face. "Calm down. I'm not going to force you."

She didn't let go of the chair. Her eyes were steady on him, like a hunted animal's.

He put his hands into his pockets and watched her quietly. "This isn't going to get us anywhere," he remarked.

She cleared her throat. "Good."

"Barrie, it's been five years," he said irritably. After the closeness they'd shared while he was in the hospital, now they seemed to be back on the old footing again. "I've been half a man for so long that it's a revelation to have discovered that I'm still capable of functioning with a woman. I only want to know that it wasn't a fluke, a minute out of time. I want to...make sure."

Her big eyes searched his. "I'm afraid of you like that."

"You weren't just after you had the nightmare," he reminded her. "You weren't the next morning. In fact, you weren't in the hospital when I let you bathe me."

Her hands released the back of the chair. Her short nails had left fine marks in the soft leather. She stared at them. "You weren't...aroused when you pulled back the sheet," she faltered.

"That's what bothers me most, that it didn't last until you tried to bathe me," he said heavily. "Maybe it was just a flash in the pan, the whole thing," he said with black humor. "But either way, I want to know. I *have* to know."

There was something in the way he looked that made Barrie feel guilty. Her own fear seemed a poor thing in comparison with the doubt in his hard face. It was devastating for a man to lose his virility. Could she really blame him for wanting to test it, to know for sure if he'd regained what he'd lost?

Slowly, hesitantly, she stepped away from the chair and let her hands fall to her sides. After all, she'd seen him totally nude, she'd felt his body against hers when it was aroused, and she hadn't succumbed to hysteria. Besides, she loved him. He was here with her, alive and vital. Her mind wouldn't let go of the picture it held—Dawson in the overturned car, his face covered with blood. She looked at him with her heart in her eyes.

His eyes traced her face in its frame of long, wavy dark hair to her soft, parted lips. His hands were still in his pockets, and he didn't move, despite the fact that her expression made him feel violent. She looked as if she cared.

"Are you just going to stand there?" she asked after a minute.

He searched her eyes. "Yes."

She didn't understand for a moment, and then he smiled faintly, and she realized what he wanted. "Oh," she said. "You want me to...kiss you."

He nodded. He still didn't move.

His lack of action made her less insecure. She moved toward him, went close, so that she could feel the heat from his tall, powerful body, so that she could smell the clean scents of soap and cologne that always clung to him. He'd shaved. There was no rasp of beard where she reached up and hesitantly touched his cheek. Involuntarily her fingers slid down to his long, firm lower lip and traced it.

His breath drew in sharply. She felt him tense, but his hands stayed in his pockets.

Curious, she let her fingers become still on his face. There was something in his eyes, something dark and intense. She searched them for a long moment, but she couldn't read the expression.

At least, she didn't understand until she took an involuntary step closer and felt his body against hers.

"No fluke," he said through his teeth. His voice sounded odd. "Now I don't want to frighten you," he continued shortly, "so if you're getting cold feet, this is your last chance to move away."

She wasn't sure if she meant to hesitate, but she did. His hands came out of his pockets and slid to cradle her by the hips. He pulled her, very gently, against him, and then moved her slowly against the raw thrust of his body, shivering.

It wasn't so frightening that way. She was fascinated by what she saw.

"Yes," he said through his teeth. "You recognize vulnerability, don't you?" he asked impatiently, hating the helpless desire he felt even while he thanked God for the ability to feel it. "My legs are shaking. Can you feel them?" He drew her a little closer, to make sure that she could. "I'm swelling. You can feel that, too, can't you?"

It was embarrassing to hear him telling her such intimate things, especially in that angry tone. She flushed, but when she tried to drop her eyes, he caught her chin and made her look at him.

"Stop cringing. I'm not a monster," he said roughly. "I lost control with you at the worst possible time, and I hurt you. I won't hurt you again."

She swallowed. The feel of his body in such close contact made her nervous, but it also excited her to feel him wanting her. She grew dizzy with confused sensations. She shifted uneasy yet exhilarated at the same time.

He drew in a sharp breath and groaned, and then he laughed. "God, that feels good!" He bit off the words. He actually shivered. His eyes met hers and he moved her against him in the same exotic little motion she'd made without thinking. His teeth ground together and the laughter came again. "I'd forgotten what it felt like to be a man."

His pleasure affected her in the oddest way. She buried her face in his chest, half afraid, half excited. She shivered, too, as his arms enfolded her.

"So you feel it, too, do you?" he asked at her ear. His hands tightened on her hips and he repeated the rough, deft motion and heard her cry out. "Do you like being helpless?" he asked, and his head bent. "Do you like wanting me and feeling powerless to draw away?"

She could hear the resentment, mingled with heated desire, in his deep voice. She opened her mouth to respond and his lips moved over it, opening to fit the shape of it before they settled with a rough, hungry, demanding pressure that made her stiffen with unexpected pleasure.

Pictures of tidal waves flew through his mind as he groaned and forced her body into even more intimacy with his. He wanted her. God, he wanted her. It was a fever that burned so high and bright that he couldn't hide his need. It grew and swelled, the pressure hard against her soft stomach. He could feel her embarrassment as she tried to move her hips away from his, but he wouldn't permit it. He couldn't. He needed her softness against the flare of his masculinity.

He needed her.

His arm forced her closer as his mouth deepened the slow kiss into stark intimacy. She felt the slow, soft penetration of his tongue, the hard caress of his lips, the aching deep groan that shuddered out of his chest.

Her arms were under his and around him. She could feel the heat from the hard muscles under her hands. She could feel his belt digging into her midriff. His powerful legs were trembling as he moved her against him and he groaned again, in anguish.

While he kissed her, his hands went deftly under the knit top to the front catch of her lacy bra, quickly loosening the catch before she could protest. His hands slowly took the weight of her bare breasts, caressing their hard tips, while the kiss went on and on. He felt her body tremble again and heard her soft cry go into his mouth. He couldn't stop. It was just like France, just like that night in her room. Some part of him stood away and saw his own helpless headlong rush into seduction, but he was too far gone to fight it now. He hadn't been a man for years. Now he was in the grip of the most desperate arousal he'd ever felt and he had to satisfy it. He wanted her, needed her, had to have her.

He was practiced, an expert in this most basic of arts. She was, for all her fears, still a novice who'd never known pleasure. He was going to give her that. He was going to make her want the satisfaction his body demanded.

Slowly he began to to slide the fabric of her blouse from her body while his mouth bit at hers in the kind of kisses that were a blatant prelude to intimacy. They threw her off-balance so that she made no protest when he removed the top and bra and dropped them onto the carpet. His hands caressed her soft, bare breasts and he drew away a breath so that he could watch them under the tender mastery of his hands.

"They're beautiful," he whispered tenderly, aware at some level of her dazed, wide-eyed stare. His hands caught her waist and he lifted her to his mouth. He traced the hard tips with soft wonder, savoring their taste with lips that cherished her. "You taste of rose petals and perfume," he breathed, nipping her tenderly.

She made a sound that brought his head up. He looked into her eyes, seeing the excitement, the shock of wonder in them. No, she couldn't stop him now. He recognized that blank, set expression on her face. She was in the throes of passion. There was no way she could draw back now, even if she'd wanted to.

Confident, he let her slide down his body and he moved back a step. She didn't try to cover her breasts. After a minute he caught the hem of his own knit shirt and pulled it over his head, tossing it onto the floor with her things.

His chest was sexy, she thought through a haze of pleasure, staring at it, bronzed and muscular with a thick curling mat of hair just a few shades darker than the hair on his head. Without volition, she moved forward and leaned into him, closing her eyes with a shaky sigh as she felt his bare chest against her breasts.

His big hands flattened just under her shoulder blades and drew her closer in erotic little motions that made her shiver.

She felt the heavy, hard beat of his heart under her ear. She traced the nipple beside her mouth and felt him tauten. Then he groaned and his mouth slid down and found hers. He lifted her clear off the floor and stood holding her, kissing her, in the middle of the sunlit room. For an instant he looked up and glared around the room. There was only the sofa or the desk or the carpet. He groaned.

He had no more time for decisions. Shaking with the terrible need to have her, he couldn't risk having her come back to her senses before...

He laid her down on the carpet in front of the picture window that overlooked the lawn half a story below. Her body, there in the light, had the shimmer of a pearl. He knelt beside her and slowly, tenderly, stripped the clothing from her body, leaving it bare and trembling, all the while tracing her softness with his lips, with his hands, in skilled caresses that made it impossible for her to draw back.

He removed his own clothes then, still a little uncertain that his body was going to cooperate with him despite its tense need. So many years, so much pain, so much hunger. He looked at her and felt his whole body clench as he stood above her, shivering a little in the fullness of his arousal.

She looked at him with faint fear in a single moment of sanity. It hadn't been this intimate before. In the darkness, she'd had hardly a glimpse of him. Now, standing over her that way, she saw the magnitude of his arousal and flushed.

"I'll be careful," he said quietly.

He eased down beside her, restraining his own desire. He smoothed the hair back from her flushed face and bent to kiss her with aching tenderness, stemming the rush of words that rose to her lips. She wanted to tell him that she was unprotected, to ask him if he was going to take precautions. But his mouth settled hard on her breast and she arched, shivering with hot pleasure, and her last grasp on reason fell away.

The slow, easy movements of his hands and mouth relaxed her. She lay watching him touch her, hearing the deep tenderness of his voice as he whispered to her. The words became indistinguishable as he touched her more intimately. Her body lifted, shivered, opened to him. Her eyes, wide with awe, sought his as the pleasure built to some unexpected plateau and trembled there on the edge of ecstasy as he moved over her at last and his body began, very slowly, to join itself to hers.

She stiffened at first, because it was suddenly difficult, and her eyes flew open, panicked.

He paused, breathing heavily, and bent to kiss her wild eyes closed. He couldn't lose control, he told himself. Not this time. He had to fight his own desperate hunger for her sake. "I won't hurt you," he whispered roughly. His hand caressed over her flat stomach, lightly tracing, soothing. "I won't hurt you, baby. Try to relax for me."

Her eyes opened again, hesitant and uncertain. "You're...so...so...!" she blustered, swallowing. "What if I can't...?"

He groaned, because he was losing control, losing it all over again when he'd sworn he wouldn't, that he could contain the raging desire she kindled. But he couldn't. The feel of her body cost him his restraint.

He moved helplessly against her. "You did before," he said. "God, Barrie, don't tense like that!" he whispered urgently. "Oh, baby, I can't stop...!" His hand suddenly slid between them and he began to touch her expertly, feeling her body respond immediately, uncoiling, lifting helplessly. "Yes!" he groaned. "Yes, yes...!" He shuddered and suddenly his tongue was in her mouth probing, like his body, teasing, penetrating...!

She sobbed. He was doing something to her, something that made a rush of pleasure shoot through her like fiery shafts, that made her body crave what he was doing, what she was feeling...

There was a fullness that grew unexpectedly, that teased and provoked and excited. She was empty and now, now, she felt the impact of the fullness, shooting through her like fireworks, making her body throb in a new rhythm, making her blood flow faster. She could hear herself breathing, she could hear him breathing, she could feel his hips moving, his skin sliding sensuously against hers, above her, as his body moved closer and closer. She couldn't breathe for the hectic beat of her heart. She opened her eyes, her nails biting into his muscular upper arms as she tried to look down, to understand what was happening to her.

"No, don't look," he snapped when she tried to see. He kissed her eyelids, so that they had to close, and his mouth found hers again. His hand was still between them, and she was feeling things so intense that they made her mind spin.

"What are you . . . doing?" she gasped against his devouring mouth, shivering as the pleasure suddenly gripped her and made her body convulse.

"My God . . . what do you think I'm doing?" he cried out, shuddering as his hips pushed down in a pressure that sent the sun shattering behind her eyelids in a burst of pleasure so primitive that she sobbed like a child.

She couldn't tell how he was touching her now, she didn't care. She was moving with him, helplessly. Her taut body felt hot and tight and swollen. She felt it opening to the fullness that was alien and familiar all at once. This, she thought blindly, must be how a man prepared a woman for his body, this . . . !

His mouth never left her own. She was buffeted in a hard, quick rhythm that increased the fullness and the pressure, and it wasn't enough to fill the emptiness she had inside. Her legs felt the rough brush of his as she heard the anguish that came gruffly from the lips possessing hers. She could hear someone pleading, a sobbing high voice that sounded oddly like her own. She went rigid as the feeling stretched her as tight as a cord and suddenly snapped in the most unbelievable rush of hot pleasure she'd ever known in her entire life.

She felt intimate muscles stretching, stretching, felt her body in rhythmic contractions that threatened to tear her apart. And even as they took her to a level of ecstasy she'd never dreamed existed, the plateau she'd reached fell away to reveal one even higher, more intense . . .

She cried out, shivering, sobbing, drowning in pleasure. She must have opened her eyes, because his face was above hers, taut and rigid, his eyes so black they might have been coals. His teeth were clenched and he was trying to say something, but he suddenly cried out and his face flooded with color. She watched him in rapt wonder, saw his eyes go black all at once, saw the helpless loss of control, the set rigor of climax that made his face clench. The pressure inside her exploded and she felt his body go rigid, convulsing under her fascinated eyes as his voice cried out hoarsely in an endless moan of pleasure. His chest strained up, away from her, his arms shivering with the convulsive pleasure. He shuddered again and again, and all the while she watched him, watched him . . .

He felt her eyes, hated them, hated her, even while the world was exploding under him. He thought he was going to faint with the onrush of ecstasy, reaching a level he'd never dared achieve before it left him helpless. Always, he'd been in control. He'd watched women in this anguished rictus, but he'd never allowed a woman to see it happen to him. Until now. He was helpless and Barrie could see. She could see . . . what he really felt. Oh, God, no . . . ! He wanted to close his eyes, but he couldn't. She could see everything . . . *everything.*

The room seemed to vanish in the violence of his rapture. It was a long time before he could open his eyes and see the carpet where his cheek lay against her body. He was shaking. Under him, he felt her labored breathing, felt her cool skin touching his, felt her hands touching his hair, heard her voice whispering shaken endearments, whispering, whispering. Damn her. Damn her!

As she held him, her breasts were wet, like the rest of her body. He was heavy, lying on her. She felt his shoulders and they were cool and damp. She moved her hands and felt his thick gold hair, wet with sweat. When she moved, she felt the pressure of him deep inside her body. She gasped.

When he could breathe completely again, he lifted his head and searched her eyes with barely contained fury at his loss of command, raising himself on both elbows so that she came into focus. He looked odd. He poised above her with a dark scowl.

His jaw tightened. "I saw you watching me," he said. "Did you enjoy it? Did it please you to watch me lose control to the extent that I couldn't even turn my face away?"

The angry words shocked her after the intimacy they'd just shared. She didn't understand the anger that flared in his face. He looked at her with contempt, almost hatred, his lips making a thin line. He took a rough breath and began to lift away, but she hated to lose the intimacy, the oneness he'd shared with her. Her body gripped him in protest at his upward movement, but then she suddenly cried out and her fingernails bit into him.

"Dawson, don't!" she whispered frantically, clutching at him.

He stopped moving at once, afraid that he'd hurt her. He scowled. "What's wrong?" he asked curtly.

Her face was rigid. She could feel the contractions inside her body. "It...hurts when you move," she said, embarrassed. She licked her dry lips. He muttered something that made her color and started to withdraw again, but this time he did it gently, with a slow, steady pressure. It was still uncomfortable, but not painful.

She looked down and blushed as red as a rose as he lifted himself completely away from her.

He rolled away from her and got to his feet, his muscles trembling from the violence of his fulfillment and the fear her cry had aroused. Memories of the night in France came back and he couldn't look at her.

He'd hurt her again. He jerked his clothes back on, hating his helplessness. He was just like his father, he thought furiously, a victim of his own uncontrollable desire. He wondered if Barrie had any idea how it frightened him to be at the mercy of a woman or why.

Barrie didn't understand his coldness, but slowly her pride came to the rescue. She couldn't bear to think of the risk she'd just taken, of the things he'd said to her. She'd welcomed him without a thought for the future, walking like a lamb into the slaughter, just as she had five years ago. Would she never learn? she wondered bitterly.

She drew herself up, wincing at the unfamiliar soreness, embarrassed and hurt as she reached for her things and began to dress, more clumsily than he had. She didn't understand what had made him so angry. He'd wanted her. Had it only been to prove his manhood after all? He'd given her pleasure that she never expected, and at first he'd been tender, almost loving. Now he wouldn't even look at her.

He was breathing a little unsteadily still. She didn't seem to be damaged, at least, thank God. But as his fear for her subsided, his anger at himself only increased. His body ached with the pleasure he'd had from her, but his pride was lacerated. He'd lost himself in her. He'd been helpless, so in thrall to desire that he'd have taken her in the hall, in the car . . .

He turned away, unable to bear even the sight of her. He was like his father. He was a slave to his desire. And she'd seen him that way, vulnerable, helpless!

She bit her lower lip until she drew blood. "Dawson?"

He couldn't look at her. He stared out the window with his hands tight in his pockets.

She felt cold. Her arms clenched around her body. It was impossible not to understand his attitude, even if she didn't want to. "I see," she said quietly. "You only wanted to know if you...could. And now that you do, I'm an embarrassment, is that it?"

"Yes," he said, lying through his teeth to save his pride.

She hadn't expected him to agree. She stared at him with eyes that had gone dark with shock. The clock had turned back to France, to that night in her hotel room. The only difference was that he hadn't hurt her this time. But she felt just as cheap, just as used, as she had then.

There was really nothing else to say. She looked at him and knew that the love she'd felt for him since her teens hadn't diminished one bit. The only difference was that now she knew what physical love truly was. She'd gloried in it, drowned in the wonder of his desire for her, given all that he asked and more. But it still wasn't enough for him. Now she knew that it never would be. He hated his hunger for her, that was obvious even to a novice, despite the fact that he'd indulged it to the absolute satiation of his senses. He wanted her, but it was against his will, just as it had been five years ago. Maybe he hated her, too, for being the object of his desire. How ironic that he was impotent with everyone else. How tragic.

She knew that it would do no good to conduct a post-mortem. He was uncommunicative, and all her efforts weren't going to dent his reserve. She turned and went to the door, unlocking it with cold hands. Even when she went through it, he never looked her way or said a single word. Nor did she expect him to. He'd frozen over.

She took a bath and changed her clothes. Her shame was so sweeping that she couldn't bear to look at herself in the mirror. There was another fact that she might have

to face. He hadn't even tried to protect her, and she'd been
so hopelessly naive as to welcome the risk of a child. If
she'd had any sense at all, she'd have let him writhe with
his insecurities about being a man. If she'd had any sense
at all, she'd have run like the wind. Which was, of course,
what she was about to do.

It only took her a few minutes to pack. She put everything into her suitcase and garment bag and carried the lot
down the staircase by herself. Rodge and Corlie were busy
with their respective chores, so they didn't see or hear her
go out the front door. Neither did Dawson, who was still
cursing himself for his lack of restraint and pride.

He didn't realize she'd gone until he heard the car en-
gine start up. He got to the front door in time to see her
turning from the driveway onto the main highway that led
to Sheridan.

For a few seconds, he watched in anguish, his first
thought to go after her and bring her right back. But what
would that accomplish? What could he say? That he'd
made a mistake? That giving in to his passion for her had
been folly and he hoped they wouldn't both live to regret
it?

He closed the front door and rested his forehead against
it. He'd wanted to know that he was still a whole man,
and now he knew that he was. But only with Barrie. He
didn't want any other woman. The desire he felt for Barrie was sweeping and devouring, it made him helpless, it
made him vulnerable. If she knew how desperately he
wanted her, she could use him, wound him, destroy him.

He couldn't give anyone the sort of power over him that
Barrie's mother had held over George Rutherford. He'd
actually seen her tease George into a frenzy, into begging
for her body. Barrie didn't know. She'd never known that
her mother had used George's desire for her to make him
do anything she liked. But Dawson knew. A woman with
that kind of power over a man would abuse it. She

couldn't help herself. And Barrie had years of Dawson's own cruelty to avenge. How could he blame her if she wanted to make him pay for the way he'd treated her?

He didn't dare let Barrie stay. She'd seen him totally at the mercy of his desire, but she didn't, thank God, know how complete her victory was. He could let her leave thinking he'd turned his back on her, and that was for the best. It would save his pride.

From his childhood, he'd known that women liked to find a weakness and exploit it. Hadn't his own mother called him a weakling when he'd begged to be held and loved as a toddler? She'd made him pay for being born. And then George had married Barrie's mother, and he'd seen the destructive pattern of lust used as a bargaining tool, he'd seen again the contempt women had for a man's weaknesses. He'd seen how his father had been victimized by his own desire and love. Well, that wasn't going to happen to him. He wasn't going to be vulnerable!

Barrie thought he'd only wanted to prove his manhood; she'd think he'd used her. Let her. She wouldn't get the chance to gloat over his weakness, as her mother had gloated over his father's. She wouldn't ever know that his possession of her today had been the most wondrous thing that had ever happened to him in his life, that her body had given him a kind of ecstasy that he'd never dreamed he was capable of experiencing. All the barriers had come down, all the reserve, all the holding back.

He'd . . . given himself to her.

His hands clenched violently. Yes, he could admit that, but only to himself. He'd gone the whole way, dropped all the pretense, in those few seconds of glorious oblivion in her arms. He hated that she'd seen his emotions naked in his eyes while he was helpless, but that couldn't be helped now. It was the first time in his life that he'd ever been able to give himself to pure physical pleasure, and it was probably only due to the enforced abstinence of sex. Yes.

Surely that was the only reason he'd had such pleasure from her.

Of course, she'd had pleasure from him, too. It touched something in him to realize how completely he'd satisfied her in spite of her earlier fear. He felt pride that he'd been able to hold back at least that far, that he'd healed the scars he'd given her during their first intimacy.

But wouldn't it be worse for her, now that she knew what kind of pleasure lay past the pain? And wouldn't she be hurt and wounded even more now by his rejection, after she'd given in to him so completely? His only thought had been for his pride, but now he had to consider the new scars she was going to have. Why hadn't he let her go while there was still time? He groaned aloud.

"Dawson?" Corlie called from the kitchen doorway. "Don't you and Barrie want any lunch?"

"Barrie's gone," he said stiffly, straightening, with his back to her.

"Gone? Without saying goodbye?"

"It was... an emergency." He invented an excuse. "A call from a friend in Tucson who needed her to help with some summer school project. She said she'd phone you later."

She hadn't said that at all, but he knew she would phone. She loved Corlie and Rodge. She wouldn't want to hurt their feelings, even if she was furious with Dawson.

"Oh," Corlie said vaguely. "I must not have heard the phone ring." She was curious about his rigid stance and the scowl between his eyes when he glanced at her, but Dawson in a temper wasn't someone she wanted to antagonize. "All right, then. Do you want some salad and sandwiches?"

He shook his head. "Just black coffee. I'll come and get it."

"You've quarreled, haven't you?" she asked gently.

He sighed heavily as he walked toward the kitchen. "Don't ask questions, Corlie."

She didn't, but it took every last ounce of her willpower. Something had gone terribly wrong. She wondered what.

Barrie, meanwhile, was well on her way back to Arizona. She stopped at the first café she came to, certain that she wouldn't have to worry about Dawson following her. The very set of his head had told her that he wouldn't.

She ordered coffee and soup and then sat barely touching it while she relived her stupidity. Would she never learn that Dawson might want her body, but never her heart? This was the second time she'd given in to him. She'd gotten pregnant the very first. Would she, from something so insanely pleasurable? It seemed almost fated that such an experience would produce a child, even if he didn't love her...

Her hand touched her flat stomach and she let herself dream for a space of precious seconds, her eyes closed. Dawson's child, in her body. It would be wonderful to be pregnant again. Somehow she'd carry the child to term. Even if she had to stay in bed forever, she wouldn't lose it...!

She opened her eyes and came back to her senses. No. She removed her hand. She was being fanciful. It wouldn't happen, and even if it did, how would she cope? Dawson didn't want her. She repeated that, refusing to recall his anguish at her loss of their first child, his hunger for a baby. She couldn't let herself dream about Dawson's reaction if he knew she was pregnant. Besides, she thought, lightning rarely struck twice.

She'd simply go back to Tucson and forget Dawson. She'd done it once before. She could do it again!

Eight

But it wasn't that easy to forget him. Barrie had started losing her breakfast the day she got back to Tucson, just as she had after that disastrous night in France. She, who never had nausea a day in her life! She'd been home for two weeks now, and it hadn't stopped. It was the absolute end, she thought as she bathed her face at the sink, the absolute end that she could get pregnant so easily with him.

Now that lightning did appear to strike twice, what in the world was she going to do?

She hadn't let any of her lukewarm suitors know she was back in town, so there were no phone calls. She didn't have to worry about a part-time job because, apparently, Dawson had settled the deal with Leslie Holton over her tract of land. He'd have those water rights and he could keep his cattle on the Bighorn land that Barrie owned with him.

Her eyes went to the emerald engagement ring he'd given her such a short time ago. She hadn't meant to take it with her, she'd meant to leave it, but she'd been upset at the time, and she'd forgotten about it. She would have to send it back. Her fingers touched the beautiful ring and she sighed as she thought about what might have been. How wonderful if Dawson had bought her a set of rings years ago, knowing that she loved emeralds, if he'd bought them with love and asked her to marry him and told her that he loved her. Oh, what lovely dreams. But it was reality she had to face now.

She curled up in an armchair, still a little nauseous, and began to make decisions. She could go on teaching, presumably, although it was going to be tricky, under the circumstances. She would be an unwed mother and that wouldn't sit well considering the profession she followed. What if she lost her job? The money she got from her share of George Rutherford's estate, while it helped make her life comfortable, was hardly enough to completely support her. She couldn't risk losing her job. She'd have to move somewhere else, invent a fictitious husband who'd deserted her, died . . . !

Her stomach churned and she swallowed a rush of nausea. How shocking to be able to tell that she was pregnant so soon after conception, she thought. But it had happened just that way after she'd returned from France. In fact, in some mysterious way, she'd known even while Dawson was taking her. Her eyes closed. Taking her. Taking her. She could feel the harsh thrust of his muscular body, feel all over again the insane pleasure that had spread into her very blood.

She made a sound deep in her throat and opened starkly wounded eyes as the knock on the door coincided with her groan.

She blinked away the memories and got up, swaying a little as she made her way to the door. She didn't want company. She didn't want to talk at all. She leaned her forehead against the cold wood and looked through the peephole. Her heart froze in her chest.

"Go away!" she cried hoarsely, wounded to the heart that Dawson should be standing there.

He looked toward the door, his face pale and set. "I can't."

That was all he said, and not very loudly, but she heard him. Surely he wouldn't know, *couldn't* know. She smiled at that naive imagining. Of course, he knew, she thought fatally as she sighed and unlocked the door. There was some mysterious mental alchemy that had always allowed them to share their thoughts.

She didn't look up as he entered the apartment, bareheaded, reserved. She closed it and turned away, to sit back down in the armchair.

He stood over her, his hands in the pockets of his gray suit and looked at her pale, pinched face. Her lack of makeup and the dark circles under her eyes told their own story.

"I know," he said uncomfortably. "God only knows how, but I do."

She looked up, her wounded eyes searching his pale, glittery ones. She shrugged and stared at her clenched hands instead. She was barefoot, wearing a loose dress instead of jeans, because of the nausea. He probably knew that, too.

He let out a long, rough sigh and sat down on the sofa opposite her, leaning toward her with his hands clasped over his knees.

"We have to make some quick decisions," he said after a minute.

"I'll manage," she said tightly.

He turned the diamond horseshoe ring on his right hand. "You're an educator. Not the most liberal of professions. You won't get that promotion. You may not even be able to keep your job, despite the enlightenment of modern life." He looked up, his pale green eyes lancing into her own. "I want this baby," he said gruffly. "I want it very much. And so do you. That has to be our first concern."

She couldn't believe this was happening, that he was so certain, that she was pregnant. "You can't tell until six weeks. It's only been two," she began, faintly embarrassed.

"We knew while we were making him," he said through his teeth. "Both of us. I didn't take precautions, and I knew without asking that you weren't using anything, either. It wasn't an accident."

She'd known that, at some level. She didn't try to deny it.

"We have to get married," he said.

She laughed bitterly. "Thanks. As proposals go, that's a honey."

His face was tight and uncommunicative. "Think what you like. I've made the arrangements and applied for the license. We'll both need blood tests. It can be done in Sheridan."

She looked up at him, her eyes furious. "I don't want to marry you," she said flatly.

"I don't want to marry you, either," he snapped right back, his face mocking and angry. "But I want that baby you're carrying enough to make any sort of sacrifice, even having to live with a woman like you!"

She jumped to her feet, her eyes flashing, her body shivering with rage, with hatred, with outrage. "If you think I'm going to...!" she shouted at him, when all at once, her face went white and she felt the nausea boiling up into her throat, into her mouth. "Oh, God!" She choked, running toward the bathroom.

She barely made it. There had been a grim satisfaction in seeing the guilt on Dawson's lean, tanned face when he realized what he'd caused. Good, she thought through waves of nausea, she hoped he suffered for it.

She heard footsteps, and then water running. A wet cloth was held against her forehead until the nausea finally passed. She was vaguely aware of him coping with his normal cold efficiency, handling everything, helping her to bathe her face and wash the taste out of her mouth. He lifted her then and carried her into the bedroom, laying her gently on the covers. He propped two pillows behind her and went away long enough to fetch a cold glass of water and help her take a sip. The cool drink settled her stomach, but she glared at him just the same.

He was sitting on the side of the bed. His lean hand went to her damp, tangled hair. He smoothed it gently away from her face and studied her features with faint guilt. He'd tried so hard to stay away, to let go. But the past two weeks had been pure torment. He'd spent them going from ranch to ranch, checking stock and books, and it hadn't helped divert him. He'd missed Barrie as never before. And in some mysterious way, he'd known there was going to be a child. That had brought him here. That, and the feelings he didn't want to have for her.

"I'm sorry," he said tersely. "I didn't mean to upset you."

"Yes, you did," she replied. "You don't want to be here at all. And I'm not marrying any man who has the opinion of me that you do!" she added hotly.

He stared at his hands for a long moment. He didn't speak. The skin of his face was pulled taut by clenched muscles.

She put her hands over her eyes with a shaky sigh. "I feel horrible."

"Were you sick like this . . . after France?" he asked.

"Yes. It started the very next morning, just like this time. That's how I knew," she said wearily. She didn't open her eyes.

He turned and looked at her, wincing at the fatigue he could see in every line of her face, in the very posture of her body. Without conscious volition, his lean hand went to her belly and pressed lightly there, through the fabric, as if he could feel the child lying there in the soft comfort of her body.

She moved her hands, shocked by the touch of his hand, and saw his high cheekbones ruddy with color as he looked at her stomach.

He felt her gaze and met it them with his own. There was no expression at all in his face, but his eyes glittered with feeling.

"Why?" she said heavily, her voice thick with tears. "Oh, why, why...?"

His arms slid under her. He lifted her across his powerful thighs and enveloped her against him, one hand pressing her cheek to his chest in a rough gesture of comfort. She cried, and he held her, rocked her. Outside were the sounds of car horns and pulsing engines and brakes and muffled voices. Inside, closer, there was the sound of her choked sobs and her ragged breathing.

"Don't," he said huskily at her ear. "You'll make yourself sicker."

Her hand clenched against his broad chest. She couldn't remember when she'd been so miserable. He'd made her pregnant and now he was going to marry her, so that their child would have the security of parents. But some part of him hated her, resented her. What sort of life would they have?

As she thought it, the words slipped out, muffled by tears.

His chest rose and fell heavily, his breath audible as it stirred her hair. "We haven't many options," he answered her quietly. His hand smoothed her disheveled hair. "Unless you want to stop this pregnancy before it begins," he added, his voice as cold as winter.

She laughed bitterly. "I can't step on an ant and you think I could..."

His thumb stopped the words. "I know you can't, any more than I can," he said shortly. "I didn't mean it."

"Then why say it?" she demanded.

He tilted her face back and looked into it pensively. "You and I are two of a kind," he said absently. "I strike out and you strike back. You've never been really afraid of me, except in one way." His eyes narrowed as she flushed. "And now you aren't afraid of me that way anymore, either, are you?" he taunted softly. "Now you know what lies beyond the pain."

She pushed at his chest, but he wouldn't let go.

Something glittered in his pale eyes, something fierce and full of contempt and anger. His hand tangled in her thick hair and clenched, pulling so that her face arched up to his.

"That hurts," she protested.

His grip loosened, but only a little. His heart was beating heavily, roughly. She could feel it against her breasts. She could feel something else as well: the involuntary burgeoning of his body and the instant response of her own to it.

He laughed bitterly as he heard her soft gasp. "I was so hot that I couldn't hold back. I couldn't protect you. I couldn't even breathe at the last." His voice grew icy with self-contempt and his hand contracted again, angrily. "I want to make you that helpless in my arms. I want to make you beg me, plead with me, to satisfy you. I want you so maddened with desire that you can't go on living if I don't take you!"

He was saying something to her. Something more than just words. She looked into his face and saw bitterness and self-contempt. And fear.

Fear!

He didn't realize what he was giving away. His anger had taken control of him. "You think you can break me, don't you?" he demanded, dropping his eyes to her mouth. "You think you can lead me around by the nose, make me do anything because I want you!"

She hadn't said a word. She was still overcome by the enormity of what she was learning about him. She didn't even protest the steely hand in her hair. She lay quietly in his embrace and just listened, fascinated.

"Well, I'm not your toy," he said harshly. "I won't come running when you call or follow you around like a whipped dog begging for favors!"

Odd, she thought, that he didn't really frighten her like this, when he looked ferocious with that scowl between his flashing eyes.

"Can't you talk?" he demanded.

"What would you like me to say?" she asked softly, searching his eyes.

The calm tone eased some of the tension from his body. His hand unclenched and he winced, as if he'd only just realized his loss of control. His jaw tautened and his breathing became deliberate at once.

"You were angry because I watched," she prompted, remembering how unduly enraged he'd been about that.

The color flared along his high cheekbones.

She saw the self-consciousness in his anger. Her hand reached up hesitantly and touched his cheek. He actually flinched.

Her whole body relaxed, forcing him to shift his weight so that he could take hers. She hung in his arms, her eyes quietly clinging to his, and her fingers went from his hard cheek down to the corner of his mouth and then lightly brushed the long lower lip.

"Why didn't you want me to look?" she asked softly.

He didn't speak. His breathing grew rough.

"For heaven's sake, isn't that what sex is all about?" she faltered. "I mean, isn't the whole point of it to let go of inhibitions and restraints with another person?"

"Not for me," he said flatly. "Not ever. I don't lose myself with women."

"No," she agreed, studying him. She could almost see the answer. "No, the whole point of the thing is to make a woman lose all her inhibitions, to humble her so that she..."

"Stop it!"

He put her aside and got to his feet, his breathing unsteady. He rammed his hands into his pockets and paced to the window, viciously pulling the curtains aside.

She sat up on the bed, propped on her hands, staring at him as all of it jelled in her mind and brought a startling, shattering conclusion.

"That's why you were so vicious to me in France," she said. "You lost control."

He drew in a breath. His fingers went white on the curtain.

"That hasn't ever happened to you, not before, not with any woman," she continued in a hushed tone, knowing it was the truth without a word from him. "And that's why you hate me."

His eyes closed. It was almost a relief to have it said, to have her know it. His broad shoulders slumped as if relieved of some monumental burden.

Barrie had to lie back against the pillows. She felt faint. He wasn't admitting anything, but she knew all the same. She knew so much about him, so many things that she understood on a less conscious level. So why hadn't she realized that it wasn't Barrie he was punishing with his cutting words? It was himself, for losing command of his senses, for wanting her so desperately that he couldn't hold back.

"But, why?" she continued. "Is it so terrible to want someone like that?"

The muscles in his jaw moved convulsively. "I came across them in the hall one day," he said in a rough whisper. "She was teasing him, the way she always teased him, taunting him with her body and then drawing back. She did that to make him give in, to make him do what she wanted."

"She?" she queried, puzzled.

He didn't seem to hear her. "That day, she wanted him to trade cars. She had her heart set on a sports car, and he wasn't ready to give up the luxury sedan he always drove. So she teased him and then told him she wouldn't give in to him if he didn't let her have her way." He let out a cold breath. "He begged her." His eyes closed. "He was crying like a little boy, begging, begging...! And in the end, he couldn't contain it, and he pushed her against the wall and..."

He leaned his forehead against the cold glass, shivering with the memory. "She laughed at him. He was all but raping her, right there in full view of the whole damn household, and she was laughing that he couldn't even make it to the bedroom." He turned, his eyes blazing in a white face. "I got out before they saw me, and then I was sick. I actually threw up. You can't imagine how I hated her."

She was getting a horrible premonition. She'd seen her mother tease George Rutherford, but only with words. And once or twice, she'd heard her mother make some remark about him. But Barrie and her mother had never been close, and she'd spent as little time at home as she could manage, first at boarding school in Virginia and then at college. She made a point of staying out of her mother's way and out of Dawson's. So she'd known very little about her mother's second marriage at all. Until now.

"It was . . . my mother," she said in a ghostly tone.

"Your mother," he said with contempt. "And my father. She treated him like some pitiful dog. And he let her!"

Her breathing was oddly loud in the sudden stillness of the room. She looked at Dawson and went white. Everything he felt, remembered, hated in all the world was in his eyes.

She understood. Finally it made some terrible sort of sense. She dropped her eyes to her lap. Poor Dawson, to have to witness something like that, to see the father he adored humiliated time and time again. No wonder he drew back from what he felt with Barrie. He didn't want to be helpless, because he didn't trust her not to treat him with the same contempt her mother had had for George Rutherford. He couldn't know that she loved him too much to want to hurt him that way. And of course, he didn't trust her, because he didn't love her. His was nothing more than a helpless physical passion without rhyme or reason, a hated weakness that he couldn't help. He looked at love as a woman's weapon.

"I'm so sorry," she said quietly. "I didn't know."

"How could you not know what she was like? She was your mother!"

"She never wanted me," she confessed stiffly, and it was the first time she'd ever talked about her mother to him, or to anyone else. Her face felt frozen. "She told me once that if abortion had been legal at the time, she'd never have had me in the first place."

He was shocked. His heavy brows drew into a frown as he looked at her, sitting as stiff as a poker in the bed. "Good God."

She shrugged. "My father loved me," she recalled with determined pride.

"He died when you were very young, right?"

"Yes," she said.

He didn't even blink. "You were sixteen when she married my father." His eyes narrowed. "How many men did she go through before she found him, Barrie?" he asked with sudden insight.

She bit her lip almost through, wincing at the pain.

"Stop biting your lips," he muttered impatiently.

She smoothed her finger over it resignedly. "She had lovers, if that's what you're asking." She glanced at him. "That's why you thought I'd had them," she realized.

He nodded. He moved to the bed and sat down in the chair beside it, fatigue in his face, in his eyes. "She was a bitch."

"Yes," she said, not offended. She searched his face, looking for weaknesses, but he was mending the wall already. "I know you loved your father."

"I tried to," he said shortly. "She came along just when he and I were beginning to understand each other. After that, he had no time for me. Not until he was dying." He looked away. He didn't want to talk about that.

She didn't push. He'd already given away more than he'd meant to, she knew.

After a minute he took a quick breath and his pale eyes searched her thin face. "You've lost weight," he remarked abruptly.

She managed a weak smile. "I started losing meals the day I left the ranch," she confessed, and flushed as she remembered the circumstances.

"I couldn't eat for the rest of the day," he recalled. He stared at the floor. "I shouldn't have let you go like that, without a word."

"What could you have said?" she asked. "I felt used . . ."

"No!" He was really angry now. "Don't you ever say anything like that to me again. Used! My God!"

"All right, cheap, then!" she countered, sweeping back an annoying strand of hair. "Isn't that how you wanted me to feel?"

"No!"

She glared at him, her lower lip trembling with emotion.

He made a curt gesture with one big hand and his lips flattened. "Damn." He leaned forward, his head bowed, his hands supporting it as he braced his elbows on his splayed thighs.

She picked at the bedspread nervously. "You only wanted to see if you were capable with a woman," she muttered. "You said so."

His hands covered his face and pushed back into his hair. "I had an orgasm," he said roughly.

She recognized the resentment in the words even though she didn't quite understand their content. "What?"

He looked up, glared up, at her. "Don't you know what it is?"

She flushed. "I read books."

"So do I," he replied, "and until France and then that afternoon, that's the only way I knew what it meant."

"You're in your mid-thirties," she said pointedly.

"I'm repressed as hell!" he snapped back. "I never liked losing control, in any way at all with a woman, so I never permitted myself to feel anything...anything like that," he added uncomfortably. His head bent. "I got by on little tastes of pleasure, now and again."

What she was hearing shocked her. He was admitting, in a roundabout way, that he'd never been completely satisfied by a woman until he'd made love to Barrie.

"Oh."

The husky little reply made his head lift. She didn't look like a cat with the cream. She didn't even look smug. She looked...

"You're embarrassed," he said unexpectedly.

She averted her eyes. "That's nothing new, with you," she muttered, and blushed even harder.

Her inhibition made him less irritable, and much less threatened. He watched her with open curiosity.

"Don't stare at me," she grumbled. "I'm not some sort of Victorian exhibit."

"Aren't you?" He leaned forward, with his arms crossed over his splayed thighs. His wavy gold hair fell roguishly onto his wide forehead, tangled from his restless fingers in it. He hadn't remembered how soft her skin was, how radiant it was at close range. It had the sheen of a pink pearl. He'd bought her a string of them once, and balked at giving them to her. They were still in the safe back in Sheridan.

"Did you have one, too?" he asked suddenly.

Nine

She didn't know how to answer that. She was intimidated and embarrassed.

He became more relaxed when he saw her expression. She still hadn't smiled, or acted as if his fall from grace in her arms had made her want to gloat.

He leaned back and crossed his legs. "Well, well," he murmured, his eyes narrowing. "What a blush. Are you embarrassed?" he added, emphasizing the word with a mocking smile.

"Yes." She bit her lip. He got up and sat down beside her, his thumb forcing her teeth away from it. His hand spread onto her cheek, gentle and caressing while he studied her pale, pinched face.

"So am I," he confessed unexpectedly. "But maybe the reason we're embarrassed is because we've never talked about being intimate with each other."

"You've already said quite enough," she muttered stiffly.

He let out an odd, amused sound. "Miniskirts," he mused, "silk hose, four boyfriends at a time, low-cut blouses. And it never occurred to me that it was all an act. You little prude."

Her eyes flashed. "Look who's calling who a prude!!" she raged at him.

His eyebrows went up. "Who, me?"

"Yes, you!" She took a shaky breath. "You gave me hell, shamed me, humiliated me, and all because I opened my eyes at the wrong time! I couldn't really see you anyway," she blurted out, "because what I was feeling was so sweet that—" She stopped in midsentence as she realized what she was admitting.

But if she was embarrassed, he wasn't. His face changed as if by magic, his body became less taut.

He drew in a quiet breath. "Thank you," he said huskily.

She didn't recognize the expression on his handsome, darkly tanned face. "What for?"

His eyes dropped to his hands. "Making the memory bearable."

"I don't understand."

He picked at his thumbnail. "I thought you watched because you wanted to enjoy seeing me helpless."

Tears stung her eyes. She'd always thought of Dawson as invincible, stoic. This man was a stranger, someone who'd known pain and grief and humiliation. She wondered if what he'd let her know about him today was only the tip of the iceberg, if there were other painful memories that went back even farther in his life. Surely it had taken more than her mother's taunts to George Rutherford to make Dawson so bitter about women and his own sexuality.

Hesitantly, she reached out and touched his hand, lightly, her cold fingers unsteady as she waited to see if she was allowed to touch him.

Apparently she was. His hand opened, his fingers curled warmly around hers and then linked slowly with them. He turned his head, searching her eyes.

"Couldn't step on an ant, hmm?" he asked absently, and his eyes softened. "I don't suppose you could. I remember you screaming when you saw a garter snake trapped under the wheelbarrow you were using in the flower beds, and then moving it so the poor thing could escape."

She liked the way it felt to hold hands with him. "I don't like snakes."

"I know."

Her fingers slowly moved against his and she lifted her eyes quickly to make sure that he didn't mind.

His lips twitched with amusement. "You're not very sure of yourself with me after all these years."

She smiled briefly. "I'm never sure how you're going to react," she confessed.

He held her eyes. "Tell me what you felt when we made love in my study."

She flushed. She tried to look away, but he wouldn't let her avoid him.

"We've gone too far together for secrets," he said. "We're going to be married. I hurt you when I pulled back. How?"

She shook her head and dropped her eyes.

"Talk to me!"

She grimaced. "I can't!"

There was a long pause. When she got the courage to look up, he was watching her with an expression she couldn't analyze.

She felt his hand still holding hers. She looked at it, admiring the long, deeply tanned fingers wrapped in her own. Her hand looked very small in that powerful grasp.

"Reassure me, then," he said quietly. "I hurt you. But it wasn't all pain, was it?"

"Oh, no," she said. "There was so much pleasure that I thought I might die of it. I opened my eyes and I saw you, but I felt just barely conscious. Then, you started to draw away and it had been so sweet that I wanted to stay that close to you, so I resisted..." She swallowed. "That's when it started to hurt."

His breath was audible. "You should have told me what you really wanted."

"I couldn't. You looked as if you hated me."

He made a sound deep in his throat. His fingers contracted around hers. "I hated myself," he said roughly. "I've hated myself since we were in France, when I went to your room and all but raped you."

"It wasn't that," she replied. "I wanted you, too. It was just that I didn't know how."

"You were a virgin." He brought her hand to his lips and touched it softly with them. "But I wanted you so desperately that I found excuses to have you."

He was afraid that he'd injured her because he'd lost control. In fact, he was afraid that he might do it again. She felt warm inside, as if he'd shared something very secret with her. And he had. Certainly his loss of control was part of the problem along with bad memories of his stepmother and how she'd humiliated his father.

She touched his wavy hair gently. "After I lost...after the baby," she said. "The doctor told me that I should have had a complete gynecological examination before I was intimate with anyone. I was very...intact."

"I noticed," he muttered. He looked down at her, enjoying the feel of her fingers against his hair. "You said that it hurt when I pulled back, Barrie."

She flushed. "Dawson, I can't talk about this!"

He bent and brushed his mouth softly over her forehead. "Yes, you can," he whispered. "Because I have to know." His cheek rested against hers as he spoke, so that she didn't have to look at him. "In the study, just at the last, when I lost control and pushed down, did it hurt you at all, inside?''

She colored at the memory of how exquisitely he'd lost control. "No."

"Thank God! I hated your mother because of what she did to my father," he said, and his lean hand brushed back her hair."But that was never your fault. I'm sorry I made you pay for something you didn't do, Barrie," he added bitterly.

"Why didn't you ever talk to me about my mother and George?"

"At first because you were so naive about sex. Then, later, I'd built too many walls between us. It was hard to get past them." He drew her hand to his chest and held it there. "I've lived inside myself for most of my adult life. I keep secrets. I share with no one. I've wanted it that way, or I thought I did." His eyes searched hers. "We'll both have to stop running now," he said abruptly. "You can't run from a baby."

She gaped at him. "Well, I like that!"

"Yes, you do, don't you?" he asked with a gentle smile. "I like it, too. What were you going to do, go away and invent a fictional husband?"

She colored. "Stop reading my mind."

"I wish I could have read it years ago," he returned. "It would have saved us a lot of grief. I still don't know why it never occurred to me that you could become pregnant after that night on the Riviera."

"Maybe I wasn't the only one trying to run," she remarked.

His face closed up. Yes, he had tried to run, tried not to think about a baby at all. Was she rubbing it in? Gloating? Surely she didn't know about his mother, did she? He started to move away, but her hands clung to him, because she knew immediately why he'd withdrawn from her.

"There's a very big difference between teasing and sarcasm," she reminded him bluntly. "Sarcasm is always meant to hurt. Teasing isn't. I'm not going to live with you if you take offense at everything I say to you."

His eyebrows went up. "Aren't you assuming a lot?"

"Not at all. You thought I was making fun of you. I'm not my mother, and you're not your father," she continued firmly. She felt belligerent. "I can't even kill a snake, and you think I could enjoy humiliating you!"

Put that way, he couldn't, either. Barrie didn't have the killer instinct. She was as gentle as her mother had been cruel. He hadn't given that much thought. Now he had to.

He sat back down again, his eyes solemn as they searched over her face. "I don't know you at all," he said after a minute. "We've avoided each other for years. As you reminded me once, we've never really talked until the past few weeks."

"I know that."

He laughed shortly. "I suppose I'm carrying as many emotional scars as you are."

"And you don't look as if you have a single one," she replied. Her eyes fixed on him. "Did you give her the silver mouse?"

He knew at once what she was referring to. He shook his head. "I keep it in the drawer by my bed."

That was surprising, and it pleased her. She smiled shyly. "I'm glad."

He didn't return the smile. "I've done a lot of things I regret. Making you look foolish over giving me a birthday present is right at the top of the list. It shamed me, that you cared enough to get something for me, after the way I'd treated you."

"Coals of fire?"

"Something like that. Maybe it embarrassed me, too. I never gave you presents, birthday or Christmas."

"I never expected them."

He touched her disheveled hair absently. "They're in my closet."

She frowned. "What's in your closet?"

"All the presents I bought you and never gave to you."

Her heart skipped. "What sort of presents?"

His shoulder lifted and fell. "The emerald necklace you wanted when you were nineteen. The little painting of the ranch the visiting artist did in oils one summer. The Book of Kells reproduction you couldn't afford the year when the traveling European exhibition came through Sheridan. And a few other things."

She couldn't believe he'd done that for her. "But you never gave them to me!"

"How could I, after the things I'd said and done?" he asked. "Buying them eased the ache a little. Nothing healed it." He picked up her hand and his thumb smoothed over the emerald ring she was wearing on her engagement finger. "I bought you this set when you left France."

That was a statement that left her totally breathless. "Why?"

"Shame. Guilt. I was going to offer you marriage."

"You never did," she whispered in anguish.

"Of course I didn't," he said through his teeth. "When I came by your apartment a week after you'd left France, a man answered the door and told me you were in the shower. He was wearing jeans—nothing else, just jeans, and he was sweating."

She wouldn't have understood that reference once. Now, remembering the dampness of her own body after Dawson's fierce lovemaking, she understood it too well.

"That was Harvey," she said miserably." He was my landlord's son at the apartment house where I lived back then. He and his brother were building cabinets in the kitchen. They took a break and while they were doing that, I had a quick shower. I'd been helping them..." She paused. "Harvey never said I'd had a visitor!"

He winced.

"You thought he was my lover," she guessed.

He nodded. "It seemed fairly obvious at the time. I went away eaten up with jealousy, believing that I'd set you off on a path to moral destruction. I was so disheartened that I flew all the way back to France."

She could have cried. If Harvey hadn't been there, if she hadn't been in the shower, if, if, if. Her face told its own story.

"You see what I meant, the morning I came to take you to Sheridan with me?" he asked quietly. "All it takes is a missed message, a lost letter, a phone call that doesn't get answered. And lives are destroyed."

He was still holding her hand, looking at the ring on her finger.

"You knew that I loved emeralds," she said softly.

"Of course I knew." He wasn't admitting how he knew, or why he'd gone to so much trouble to find a wedding set exactly like that one.

Suddenly she remembered. "I saw a ring like this in a magazine, one of those glossy ones," she recalled. "I left it open on the sofa, to show Corlie, because I loved it so much. That was about the time I left for college."

"You had on a pink tank top and cutoffs," he recalled. "You were barefoot, your hair was halfway down your back. I stood in the doorway and watched you sprawled on the carpet with that magazine, and I had to get out of the house."

She searched his eyes. "Why?"

He gave a short laugh. "Can't you guess? Because the same thing happened that always happened when I get close to you. I got aroused."

"But you acted as if you couldn't bear the sight of me!" she blurted.

"Of course I did! I'd have given you the perfect weapon to use against me if I'd let you know how I felt!" he replied without thinking.

He really believed that. She could see it in his pale eyes as they searched her face. He'd spent all those long years protecting himself, avoiding intimacy or even affection because he thought of it as a weakness that any woman would exploit. It was no wonder that they called him the "ice man." In so many ways, he was. She wondered if anything would thaw him out. Perhaps the baby would be a start. *The baby!* With wonder, her hands went absently to her flat stomach.

The involuntary action brought Dawson out of his unpleasant memories. He followed the motion of her hands and the bitterness left his face.

He reached out and placed one of his big hands over both of hers. "I'll take care of you this time," he said quietly, "even if it means hiring a hospital staff and keeping you in bed for the full nine months."

Her hands slid over his and rested there. "I won't lose this one," she said with certainty.

He made an odd sound and there was a glimmer of real affection in his eyes. "I still can't quite believe it," he said with poignant hesitation.

"Neither can I. Well, so much for that promotion," she murmured dryly. "I'm not living in Tucson alone."

He cocked an eyebrow. "You can teach in Sheridan."

"When he starts school," she agreed.

He searched her eyes. "He?"

"I hate dolls," she murmured shyly. "But I love football and baseball and soccer and wrestling."

He chuckled with genuine amusement. "Chauvinist."

"I am not. I wouldn't mind a daughter, really. I think Antonia's stepdaughter, Maggie, is precious. I'm sure they're as crazy about her as they are about their new son, Nelson." She shrugged. "Besides, Maggie hates dolls, too.

But she loves to read and she knows almost as much about cattle as her dad.''

"I like Antonia," he replied.

"You can get used to Powell. Can't you?" she coaxed.

He pursed his lips. "I don't know. Will you make it worth my while?" he murmured with a slow, steady appraisal of her relaxed body.

She couldn't believe she was hearing that. It was the first time in memory that he'd actually teased her. He even looked rakish, with his disheveled wavy gold hair on his forehead and his pale green eyes affectionate. He was so handsome that he took her breath away, but she'd have loved him if he'd been the ugliest man on earth.

"I've shocked you," he mused.

"Continually, ever since you walked in the door," she agreed. She smiled up at him. "But to answer the question, yes, when I feel better, I'll do my best to make it worth your while."

"No more fear?" he asked, and was solemn.

"I don't think so," she replied. "If it's going to be like last time from now on. And if you won't get furious afterward again."

He took her hand in his and held it tightly. "I'll make sure it's like the last time. As for getting upset . . ." He grimaced. "It's difficult for me."

"Because you don't trust me yet," she said perceptively. "I know. You'll just have to learn how, I suppose. But I don't think making fun of people is any way to carry on a relationship, if it helps. And I don't think less of you for enjoying what we do together." She blushed. "In bed, I mean."

"We didn't do it in bed. We did it on the carpet." His face hardened. "Like animals . . ."

She sat up and put her hand over his lips. "Not like animals," she said. "Like two people so hungry for each other that they couldn't wait. There's nothing to be ashamed of in that."

He took a deliberate breath, but his eyes were still full of storms and bitterness.

She traced his long, sensuous mouth with her forefinger. "I'm sorry that my mother made you hate what you feel when we're together, Dawson," she said quietly. "But I'm not like her, you know. I couldn't hurt you. I couldn't even tell you about the baby we lost, because I knew it would devastate you."

He reached for her roughly and enveloped her bruisingly close against him. There was a fine tremor in his arms as he buried his face in the thick hair at her throat.

She smoothed his hair with gentle hands, nestling closer. "But we won't lose this one, my darling," she whispered. "I promise you, we won't."

There was a stillness in him all at once. He didn't lift his head, but his breathing was suddenly audible. "What did you call me?" he whispered gruffly.

She hesitated.

"What?" he persisted.

"I said . . . my darling," she faltered self-consciously.

He drew back enough to let him see her flushed face. "No!" he said quickly. "Don't be embarrassed! I like it."

"You do?"

He began to smile. "Yes."

She sighed with pure delight as she looked at him.

He studied her flushed face in its frame of disheveled dark, wavy hair. His hands gathered it up and tested its silkiness with pleasure that was visible. "Feeling better?"

She nodded. "I'm a little queasy, but it's natural."

"My doctor can probably give you something for it."

She shook her head. "No. I won't even take an aspirin tablet while I'm carrying him. I won't put him at the slightest risk."

He dropped his eyelids so that she couldn't see the expression in his eyes. "Do you want the baby because of that maternal instinct, or do you want him because he's my child?"

"Are you going to pretend that you don't know?" she mused. "You used to taunt me about how I felt—"

"Yes, I knew." He interrupted curtly and met her eyes. "It hurt, damn it. I was cruel to you and even that didn't make any difference. You can't imagine what torment it was to know that all I had to do was touch you and I could have you, any time I wanted to. But I had too much honor to do it." His eyes narrowed with pain. "All the same, I hope I haven't killed that feeling in you. I don't know much about love, Barrie. But I want you to love me, if you can."

Tears burned in her eyes as she felt his lips touch her forehead, her eyebrows, her wet eyelids. The tears fell and she couldn't seem to stop them. "I've loved you since the first time I saw you," she whispered unsteadily. "So much, Dawson. So much, so much...!"

He kissed her. His mouth was hungry at first, insistent, almost cruel in its devouring need. But he felt her weakness and his arms loosened their tight grip. His mouth became caressing, tender.

When he lifted his head, he looked dazed. This was his woman. She loved him. She had his child under her heart. She was going to be his wife. He felt as stunned as he looked.

"We can...if you want to," she murmured sheepishly. "I mean, I'm not that sick."

He smoothed back her damp hair. "I wouldn't be much of a man if sex was all I had in mind right now," he replied quietly. "You're carrying my child. I could burst with pride."

It was an odd way to put it, but it touched her. She smiled shyly. "One time and I'm pregnant," she said pensively. "If we don't want twenty kids, I suppose one of us is going to have to do something after the baby comes."

"I'll do something," he said. "I don't want you taking anything that might put you at risk."

"I don't have to take something. I can use something."

"We'll see."

She touched his face, his shoulder, his chest. "I could get drunk on this."

"On what?"

"On being able to touch you whenever I want to," she said absently, unaware of the effect the words had on the man holding her. "I used to dream about it."

"Even after France?" he asked with sudden bitterness.

"Even after France," she confessed. She looked up. "Oh, Dawson, love is the most stubborn emotion on earth."

"It must be," he said.

She leaned forward and kissed his eyelids closed. "When do you want to leave for Sheridan?"

"Now."

"Now? But . . . !"

"I want to get married," he said firmly. "I want to do it quickly, before you change your mind."

"But, I wouldn't!"

He wasn't sure of that. He'd made so many stupid mistakes already that he couldn't risk another one. "And we won't sleep together again until the ring is on your finger," he added.

"Why, you blackmailer," she said.

He cocked an eyebrow. "I beg your pardon?"

"Withholding your body to make me marry you. Well, I never!"

"Yes, you did," he murmured.

She liked the way his eyes twinkled when he was amused. She smiled. He might not love her, but he liked her, and he wanted her.

"Yes, I did," she agreed. "Okay, if you're in such a hurry to give up your freedom, who am I to stand in your way? I'll pack right now!"

Ten

Corlie wasn't at all surprised to see Dawson walk in with a radiant Barrie. She hugged them both and went away with a smug expression to make them a pot of coffee.

"Coffee," Barrie began. "I really should have milk…"

Dawson put his finger over her lips and looked sheepish. "Don't. I'll go and tell her we both want milk."

"She'll be even more suspicious of that," she whispered.

He shrugged. "Maybe I'm overreacting. Maybe you are, too," he continued. "We don't even know for sure yet."

She leaned into his body with her eyes closed, feeling secure and at peace for the first time in years. "Yes, we do," she said.

He rocked her in his arms. "Yes, we do," he agreed after a minute. He closed his own eyes and refused to give in to the fear. It would be wonderful to have a child with her. Surely nothing would go wrong, as it had with his mother. And she wasn't going to make him jump through hoops. His eyes opened and he stared past her. He felt troubled and turbulent. Trust came hard to a man with his history. He didn't know how he was going to cope with what lay ahead.

They were married quietly in the local Methodist church with Corlie and Rodge for witnesses. Antonia Long and her husband sent flowers and congratulations, but the baby had a cold and they wouldn't leave him, even for such a momentous occasion as to see Barrie and the "ice man" get married.

Dawson kissed her with a tenderness she'd never expected from him and Barrie felt on top of the world. Since their return to Sheridan, he hadn't touched her except to hold her hand or brush a light kiss across her mouth.

But tonight was their wedding night. She marveled at her excited anticipation, remembering the pleasure his body had taught hers to feel. It wasn't fear she was feeling now when she thought of lying in Dawson's arms in the darkness. And surely, after the honesty he'd shown her about his past, they could cope with his emotional scars. If he wanted to make love with the lights out, to conceal his vulnerability, she wouldn't even mind that. She only wanted to lie in his arms and love him.

But if she expected the wedding band to make an immediate difference in their relationship, she was in for a shock. Because that afternoon Dawson, who'd been restless and prowling ever since the reception, suddenly packed a bag and announced that he just had to see a man in California about a seed bull.

"On our wedding day?" Barrie exclaimed, aghast.

He looked more uncomfortable than ever. "It's urgent. I wouldn't go otherwise. He's threatening to sell it to someone else."

"You could just buy it," she suggested.

"Not without seeing it first." He closed his bag. "It won't take long. A few days."

"*Days?*"

He grimaced at her expression. He tried to speak and made a curt gesture with one hand instead. "I won't be away long. Corlie's got the number where I can be reached if you need me."

"I need you already. Don't go."

He paused to tilt her face up to his worried eyes. "I have to." He ground out the words.

She had a feeling that the confinement of marriage was already making him nervous. He'd faced so many things in the past few weeks, including a sudden marriage and a pregnancy. He was trapped and straining at the ropes. And if she didn't let him go now, she might lose him for good. She was wise enough to know that he needed a little time, a little room. Even if it was on their wedding day. She couldn't corner him. She had to let go.

"Okay." She smiled instead of arguing. "If you have to go, you have to go."

He seemed surprised at her lack of protest. His impatience to leave lessened. "You don't mind?"

"Yes, I mind," she said honestly. "But I understand, perhaps better than you realize."

He glared at her. "It's only a business trip. It has nothing to do with our marriage or the baby."

"Of course not."

He didn't like the expression in her eyes. "You think you know everything about me, don't you?"

Her eyebrows raised. "I haven't even scratched the surface, yet."

"I'm glad you realize it."

She reached up and kissed him beside his mouth, very gently, feeling his tall body tense at the unexpected caress. "Do you mind if I kiss you goodbye?" she asked.

He stared at her. "No."

She grinned. "Have a safe trip. Are you taking the Learjet or a commercial flight?"

"Commercial," he said surprisingly. "I don't feel like worrying with maps and vectors today."

"Good. As long as you don't feel compelled to tell the pilot how to fly," she added tongue in cheek, remembering an incident in the past when Dawson had actually gone into the cockpit to instruct the pilot to change his altimeter.

He averted his eyes. "He was a novice commuter pilot and he was so nervous that he had his altimeter set wrong. Good thing I noticed. He'd have crashed."

"I suppose he would have, at that. And he never flew again, either."

"He realized he wasn't cut out for the stress of the job, and he had the guts to admit it." He looked down at her with calmer eyes, searching over her face. "You look better than you did in Tucson," he said. "But don't overdo, okay?"

"Okay."

"And try to eat more."

"I will."

"Don't drive anywhere unless Rodge and Corlie know where you're going."

"Okay."

"And if something goes wrong, call me. Don't try to handle it yourself."

"Anything else?"

He began to look uncomfortable. "Stay away from the horses. You shouldn't go riding until we know for certain."

"You're a case," she murmured with twinkling eyes. "Imagine that, you worrying about me."

He didn't react with humor, as she'd expected. In fact, he looked more solemn than ever. He took a long strand of her hair and tested its soft texture, looking at it instead of her while he spoke. "I've always worried about you."

She sighed, admiring his rare good looks in the tan suit he wore. "I can't believe that you actually belong to me, now," she reminded him, noting his shocked expression.

It should have pleased him to hear the note of possession in her voice. It didn't. Combined with his fears of being vulnerable in her arms, it made him angry. He dropped her hair and moved away. "I'll phone you tonight. Stay out of trouble."

She colored at the snub, because that's what it was. She wasn't through walking on eggshells with him, she realized at once. She'd only just begun.

"Dawson?"

He paused, looking back with obvious reluctance.

She hesitated, frowning. She was going to have trouble approaching him at all from now on. She had to do it right the first time.

"Marriage doesn't just happen," she said, choosing her words carefully. "It takes some cooperation, some compromise. I'll go halfway, but no further."

He looked puzzled. "What do you mean?"

"You're my husband," she said, tingling as she said the word.

"And now you think you own me, because I married you?" he asked in a dangerously soft tone.

Her face felt tight. She just stared at him for a minute before she spoke. "Just remember that I didn't ask you to marry me," she said quietly. "It was *you* who came after *me*. Not the reverse."

His eyebrows rose at the haughty tone. "I came after you to save you from an unwed pregnancy," he informed her with a mocking smile. "Or did you think I had other motives? Do I look like a man who's dying for love of you?" he added with biting sarcasm.

"Of course not," she said in a subdued tone. "I know that you don't love me. I've always known."

He didn't understand the need he felt to cut her, especially now. He'd drained all the joy out of her green eyes, all the pleasure out of her radiant face. She looked tired. If she really was pregnant, as they suspected, upsetting her was the very last thing he should be doing. But she had him now, and he burned for her. He wanted her with a headlong, reckless passion that could place him forever in her power. And that wasn't the only fear he was nursing. He had cold feet and they were getting colder by the minute. He had to get away now, to be alone so that he could get a grip on himself. Dear God, why did she have to look that way? Her very silence made him feel guilty.

Her chin lifted and she managed a smile. "Have a good trip."

His eyes narrowed. "You won't run away while I'm gone?" he asked abruptly, and watched her face color. "Damn it . . . !"

"Don't you swear at me!" she snapped back. Her lower lip was trembling, her hands clenched at her sides, her eyes glittered with tears of anger and hurt. "And I'm not the one who's running, you are! You can't bear the thought of a wife, can you, especially me!"

Her loud voice brought Corlie into the hall. The housekeeper stopped dead, aghast at the scene before her eyes. There was Dawson with a suitcase, looking as unapproachable as she'd ever seen him, and Barrie crying, shivering.

"You've only just got married," she said hesitantly, looking from one of them to the other.

"Why don't you tell her the truth, Dawson? We didn't get married for love. We got married because we had to!" Barrie sobbed. "I'm pregnant, and it's his fault!"

Dawson's face went white as the words stabbed him like a knife right out of the past. He was oblivious to Corlie's shocked expression as he glared at Barrie. "Don't make it sound like that. You couldn't possibly know for sure yet!" he snapped at her.

"Yes, I could," she said in a ghostly tone. "I used one of those home pregnancy kits, and it says I am!" she growled.

Thinking it was one thing. Hearing it, knowing it, being sure—that was something entirely different. He stood with the suitcase in his hand and he didn't move. She was really pregnant. His eyes went to her stomach, where one of her hands was flattened protectively, and then back up to her hurt, wet face. But he wasn't seeing Barrie. He was seeing his mother, blaming him for her marriage, blaming him, and then at the last, in the casket, with the little casket beside her...

"Well, you're married," Corlie said, trying to find a glimmer of optimism. "And you both love children . . ."

Barrie wiped her wet eyes. "Yes, we love children." She glared at Dawson. "What are you waiting for? There's a bull standing in a pasture in California just dying for you to rush out there and buy him, isn't there? Why don't you go?"

Corlie glanced at him. "You're going to California to buy a bull on your wedding day?" she asked, as if she couldn't have heard right.

"Yes, I'm going to buy a bull," he said belligerently. He slammed his hat on his head, ignoring his guilt at the way Barrie looked. "I'll be home in a few days."

He stalked to the front door and jerked it open. He knew both women were watching him, and he didn't care. He wasn't going to go rushing to Barrie's bed like a crazed animal begging for favors, and she needn't expect it. She had to learn right from the beginning that he had the upper hand, and that he wasn't going to be some sort of sexual toy for her. She already blamed him for getting her pregnant, for ruining her life. She was going to be like his mother, she was going to torment him. He had to escape while he could.

That he was behaving irrationally didn't even occur to him. Not then, at least.

But by the time he was ensconced in his California hotel suite, the world seemed to snap quite suddenly back into focus.

He looked around him with vague shock. He'd walked out on his wife of two hours, left her alone and pregnant, to go and buy a bull. He couldn't believe what he'd done, what he'd said to her. He must have been out of his mind.

Perhaps he really was, he thought. He'd tortured himself with thoughts of making love to Barrie, but once again he'd have to submit to the madness she created in his body. He'd be helpless, vulnerable, weak. She'd watch him . . . she'd see not only his surrender to her body, but what he really felt. In the heat of ecstasy he wouldn't be able to hide it from her.

He took a long breath. He'd never faced his own vulnerability with her. In fact, he'd gone to extreme lengths to make sure he didn't have to face it. It had been impossible for him to lower the barriers between them, for fear that she'd want revenge even now for the way he'd treated her. If he let her see the extent of his desire, she'd use it against him. Hadn't his own mother taunted him with his childish weaknesses, ridiculed him, made him look small in front of his father and his friends? Hadn't she pointed out that he was a sissy because he'd cried when his German shepherd had been hit by a car? Hadn't she spent his childhood making fun of him, making him pay, unbeknownst to his father, for a marriage she'd never wanted in the first place? Dawson had been a mistake, she often told him, and she'd had to marry a man she didn't really love because of it . . .

Funny that he hadn't let himself remember those words until today. Barrie was pregnant and she'd cried that she'd had to marry Dawson because of it. If she hadn't said that, he'd never have gone out the door. Ironic that her own mother had said the same thing about her, he thought, recalling what she'd told him in Tucson. Maybe women didn't really want babies at all except as a means of torturing men and making them feel guilty. He wondered if that thought was quite coherent.

He sprawled on the luxurious sofa in the sitting room, remembering other things, remembering Barrie's soft skin under his, her sweet cries of passion as he drove her into the carpet beneath the heated thrust of his body. He groaned aloud as the memory of the ecstasy she'd given him poured into his mind and made him shiver. Could he live without ever again knowing that pleasure, regardless of the price?

His eyes closed as he lay back. He could always turn out the lights, he thought with dry humor. Then she couldn't look at him. It wouldn't matter if she heard him. He'd hear her, too. She was none too quiet when they made love. His eyes blazed with feeling as he recalled her own shocked pleasure that morning on the carpet. She'd known only pain from him before. He'd taught her that she could expect far more than that.

She'd said she loved him. Good God, how could she love him, when he kept pushing her away? Why couldn't he accept her love, why couldn't he accept his own addiction to her? She was pregnant, and he'd left her in Sheridan on their wedding day out of nothing more than cold fear because he . . . because he . . .

He opened his eyes and took a slow, painful breath. Because he loved her. There. He couldn't admit it to her, but he couldn't hide it from himself. He loved her. He'd loved her since she was sixteen, since she'd given him a silver mouse on his birthday. He'd loved her in France, hated himself for taking advantage of what she felt for him in an attempt to deny that love. But it had grown and grown until it consumed him. He couldn't get rid of it. He couldn't stop. He couldn't give in to it. What was he going to do?

Well, he thought as he managed to get to his feet, there was one thing he could do. He could have a drink, and then he was going to call Barrie and set her straight on a few things!

Barrie was surprised when she heard Dawson's thick voice on the telephone. She hadn't really expected him to call after the furious way he'd left. She'd spent the rest of the day alternately crying and cursing, while Corlie did her best to comfort and reassure her. She'd gone to bed early, sick and disappointed because her new husband couldn't even stand to be in the same house with her. And after the tenderness she'd felt in him in Tucson, too. It had been utter devastation.

Now, here he was on the phone trying to talk to her, and unless she missed her guess, he was blind, stinking drunk!

"Did you hear me?" he demanded. "I said, from now on, we're only going to make love in the dark!"

"I don't mind," she said, confused.

"I didn't ask if you minded," he muttered. "And you can't look at me while we do it."

"It would never occur to me," she said placatingly.

"And don't say you own me. You don't own me. No woman is going to own me."

"Dawson, I never said that."

"You said I belonged to you. I'm not a dog. Did you hear me?"

"Yes, I heard you." She smiled to herself at his efforts to enunciate properly. The anguish and disappointment of the afternoon had vanished as he poured out his deepest fears without even realizing it. It was a fascinating glimpse at the real man, without the mask.

"I don't belong to you," he continued. He felt hot. He pushed back his hair. He was sweating. Maybe he should turn on the air conditioner. If he could only find it. He bumped into the table and almost upset the lamp. In the tangle, he dropped the phone.

"Dawson?" Barrie called, concerned when she heard the crash.

There were muttered, half-incoherent curses and a scrambling sound as he retrieved the receiver. "I walked into the table. And don't laugh!"

"Oh, I wouldn't dream of it," she assured him.

"I can't find the air conditioner. It must be in this room somewhere. How the hell can they hide something that big?"

She almost lost it then. She had to stifle a burst of laughter. "Look under the window," she instructed.

"What window? Oh, that one. Okay."

There was another pause and some odd sounds, followed by a curse and a thud. "I think I turned on the heat," he said. "It's hot in here."

"You might call housekeeping and ask them to check," she said hesitantly.

"Check what?"

"The air conditioner."

"I already checked it," he muttered. "It's under the window."

She wasn't going to argue. "Did you see the bull?" she asked.

"What bull?" There was a pause. "Listen, there's no bull in here, are you crazy? This is a hotel!"

By now, Barrie was rolling on the floor.

"Are you laughing?" he asked furiously.

"No," She choked. "I have a cough. I'm coughing." She coughed.

There was another pause. "I was going to tell you something," he said, trying to focus. "Oh, I remember.

Listen here, Barrie, I can live without sex. I don't even need it.''

"Yes, Dawson," she agreed gently.

"But if you want to sleep with me, you can," he continued generously.

"Yes, I would like that, very much," she said.

He cleared his throat. "You would?"

"I love sleeping with you," she said softly.

He cleared his throat again. "Oh," he said after a minute.

The opportunity was too good to miss. He was talking to her as if he'd had truth serum. "Dawson," she began carefully, "why did you go to California?"

"So I wouldn't make love to you," he said drowsily. "I didn't want you to see . . . how much I wanted to. How much I cared."

Her heart began to swell, to lift, to soar. "I love you," she whispered.

He sucked in a sharp breath. "I know. I love you, too," he said drowsily. "Love you . . . so much. So much, Barrie, so much, so much . . . !" He swallowed. He couldn't quite talk.

Which was just as well, because Barrie was as speechless as he was. She gripped the receiver like a life jacket, staring into space with her heart in her mouth. "But I don't want you to know it," he continued quite clearly. "Because women like having weapons. You can't know how I feel, Barrie," he continued. "You'd torment me with it, just like your mother tormented George because he wanted her so much."

She felt the pain right down to her toes. She'd never known these things about Dawson.

"Listen, I have to go to bed now," he said. He frowned, trying to remember something. "I can't remember why I called you."

"That's all right, darling," she said softly. "It doesn't matter."

"Darling," he repeated slowly. He took a heavy breath. "You don't know how it hurts when you call me 'darling.' I'm buried inside myself. I can't dig my way out. I miss you," he whispered, his voice husky and deep. "You don't know how much. Good night . . . sweetheart."

The line went dead. Barrie stayed on it, waiting. After a minute the switchboard came on the line. She heard the operator's voice with a sense of fate. She smiled.

"May I help you?" the operator repeated.

"Yes, you may. Can you tell me how to get to your hotel?"

Corlie muttered all the way to the airport in Sheridan, but she was smiling just the same. She put Barrie on the commuter flight to Salt Lake City, Utah, where she caught the California flight. It was tiring and she was already fatigued, but it seemed somehow the right thing to do, to get to her reluctant husband before he sobered up completely.

She arrived at the hotel very early the next morning and showed the hotel clerk her marriage license. It didn't take much persuasion after that to coax him into letting her have a key to Dawson's room.

Feeling like a conspirator, she let herself in and looked around the suite with a little apprehension. But timidity hadn't brought her this far; courage had.

She opened the door to what must be the bedroom, and there he was, sprawled nude on the covers, as if he'd passed out before he could get under them. Not that he needed to. Bread could have been baked on the floor, judging by the temperature.

Barrie went to the air conditioner and found the switch turned off. She clicked it on high and cool air began to blow in. She stood there for a minute, because she was feeling a little nauseous from the heat. As the cool air filtered up to her face, she began to breathe more easily.

There was a sound and when she turned, Dawson was propped on one elbow, watching her through bloodshot eyes.

Eleven

──────

"**G**ood morning," she said, shy now that she was actually facing him after their extraordinary conversation of the previous night.

"Good morning." His eyes searched over her body in jeans and a tank top with a lined jacket over it. Her long hair was a little disheveled, and she looked flushed. He still wasn't certain that she wasn't a mirage. He scowled. "What are you doing here?"

"Turning on the air-conditioning," she said.

He cocked an eyebrow. "Pull the other one."

She lifted her chin and colored a little as her eyes registered his blatant masculinity. He wasn't only nude, he was already aroused, and apparently not the least shy anymore about letting her see. "I'm getting educated."

He smiled mockingly. "We're married. If you don't want to look at me, nobody's making you."

She glared at him. The wall was back up. She'd come all this way on hope, exhilaration that he'd finally admitted his feelings for her, only to find that she'd overstepped her limit again. He wasn't going to admit anything. He was going to go right on keeping her at a distance, refusing to let her see into his heart. The baby wouldn't make any difference. They'd live together like strangers with the child as their only common ground. She could see down the long, lonely years of loving without any visible return of her feelings for him, without hope.

"I came to tell you that I'm going back to Tucson," she said coldly. "That's what you want, isn't it?" she added when he looked shocked. "That's what this trip is all about. You married me because you felt you had to, but now you're sorry and you don't want me around. I make you lose control, and you can't stand that." She straightened. "Well, no more worries on that score. I've got my bags packed and I'll be out of your house by tomorrow!"

He threw his legs off the bed and got up. Nude, he was more than intimidating. He moved toward her and abruptly lifted her up in his arms, turning to carry her back to bed.

"Put me down!" she snapped at him. "What do you think you're doing?"

"I'll give you three guesses." He tossed her onto the bed and followed her down, catching her flailing hands. He pressed her wrists into the mattress and poised there above her, his eyes pale and steady and totally unreadable.

"I hate you!" she said furiously. Her eyes stung with unshed tears as he blurred in her vision. "I hate you, Dawson!" she sobbed.

"Of course you do." His voice sounded almost tender, she thought through the turmoil of emotions. But surely it wasn't. His hands slid up to melt into hers, tangling with her fingers as he bent and drew his lips softly, tenderly, over her mouth. His chest eased down, his long legs slid against hers in a silence that magnified her ragged breathing and the sound of his body moving against hers.

He drew her arms around his neck. His hands slid under her, disposing of catches and buttons and zippers. In a melting daze, she felt him undressing her, and all the while, his mouth was making her body sing. He nuzzled her breasts, tasting their hard tips, suckling them, while he removed the layers of fabric until she was as nude as he was. The thick hair on his chest tickled her skin at first, and then made her body tauten with desire.

He never spoke. He kissed her from head to toe, in ways he never had before, his hands touched her with a mastery that would have made her insanely jealous of the women he'd learned it with if she'd been able to think at all. His mouth teased and tempted and finally devoured hers. And all the while, he caressed her as if her pleasure was the most important thing in the world to him. He kindled fires and all but extinguished them over and over again until she was on the edge of madness, sobbing aloud for relief from the tension his expert caresses built in her.

But it was a long, long time later before he finally eased down between her legs and very gently probed the dark, sweet mystery of her body, covering her mouth with his just as he pushed softly and felt her open to absorb him.

She stiffened just a little, but there was no resistance at all to his passage, and he shifted just enough to make her gasp and cling to him before he probed even deeper. All the while, he was tender as he'd never been in the past, slow and quiet and utterly loving. *Loving.* She didn't open her eyes once. She didn't try to look at him. She lay drowning in the pleasure each slow, soft movement of his hips created, sobbing rhythmically under the exquisite throb of pleasure that grew deeper and deeper, like a drum beating in her body, beating, beating . . .

With maddening precision he built the pleasure to a crescendo that left her whimpering like a wounded thing, clinging fiercely, whispering things to him in her need that would shock her minutes later. But for now, there was no future, no shame. She pleaded helplessly, her whole body rising, shivering in a painful arch, a silent plea for fulfillment. And recognizing the end of her endurance, he moved sharply, suddenly, into complete possession in a slow, deep, endless rhythm that sent her spinning right up into the sun. Her nails bit into his back helplessly as she shuddered, sobbing under his mouth, crying out in anguished delight, tears raining down her cheeks as she endured the most incredible ecstasy she'd ever felt, so deep and throbbing that it was almost pain.

Only then, only when he felt her body convulse in the final spasms of completion did he drive fiercely for his own fulfillment. It was as before, spasms of aching pleasure that built and built and suddenly blazed in his taut body in an explosion of heat and light, making him mindless, shapeless, formless. He was part of her, as she was part of him. There was nothing in the world, only the two of them. Only... this... !

He saw the ceiling without seeing it. He was lying on his back, still trembling from the violence of his satisfaction. He could hear Barrie breathing raggedly. He could feel the dampness of her body where it lay so close and so far from his.

"They say that muscular contractions that violent could break bones without the narcotic of ecstasy to make them bearable," he remarked drowsily when he had his breath back.

She didn't say anything. She was lying on her stomach, half-dead with pleasure and so miserable that she wanted to hide. Sex. Only sex. He hadn't said a word, all the while, and now he was treating her to a scientific explanation of sexual tension.

He rolled over onto his side and looked at her. She averted her face, but he pulled her against him and tilted her chin up.

"Well, do you still want to leave me after *that?*" he asked. "Or would you like to try and convince me that all those outrageous, shocking things you whispered to me were the result of a bad breakfast...Barrie!"

She'd torn out of his arms in a mad dash for the bathroom, and only barely made it in time. She knelt there, her heart breaking in her chest, her eyes red with tears, while she lost her breakfast and everything in between. *The monster!* The monster, taunting her about a response she couldn't help! And where had he learned such skills anyway, the licentious, womanizing...!

While she was thinking it, she was saying it.

Dawson wrapped a towel around his waist and with a resigned sigh, he wet a facecloth and knelt beside her. When the nausea finally passed, he bathed her face and carried her back to bed, tucking her gently under the sheet.

"I want my clothes." She wept. "I can't leave like this!"

"No problem there. Because you aren't leaving." He picked up her clothes, opened the window and threw them out.

She lay in a daze, watching him perform the most irrational act of their long acquaintance. She actually gasped out loud.

He calmly closed the window. Below there was a loud squeal of brakes. He cocked an eyebrow at her. "That lacy bra probably landed on some poor soul's windshield and shocked him into panic," he mused. "You shouldn't wear things like that in your condition, anyway. It's scandalous."

She held the sheet tucked against her while she struggled with the possibility that Dawson's mind had snapped.

He laughed softly as he stood over her, the towel just barely covering his lean hips. Her expression amused him. "What's the matter?" he asked.

Her hand clenched on the cool cotton fabric. "I didn't bring a change of clothes," she said stiffly. "And now even my underwear—my underwear, for God's sake!—is out there being handled by total strangers! How am I supposed to leave the room, much less the hotel?"

"You aren't," he replied. His eyes slid over her soft, faintly tanned shoulders and he smiled. "God, you're pretty," he said. "You take my breath away without your clothes."

She didn't say anything. She wasn't sure it would help the situation.

He sat down beside her with a rueful smile. "I guess I can't expect you to understand everything at once, can I?" He smoothed back her hair and his eyes were tender on her pale face. "While you're struggling with your situation, I'll have them send up something to settle your stomach. How about some strawberry ice cream and melon?"

Her favorite things. She hadn't realized that he knew. She nodded slowly.

"And some hot tea."

"The caffeine..."

"Cold milk," he amended, smiling.

She nodded again.

He picked up the phone, punched room service and gave the order. Then he went to his suitcase and pulled out one of his nice, clean shirts and laid it on the bed within reach. "I don't wear pajamas," he said. "But that will make you decent when room service comes."

"How about you?" she asked uncomfortably.

He gave her a rueful look. "No guts?" he chided. "Don't want to be seen with a naked man, even if you're married to him?"

She flushed.

"And you were calling me a prude." He got up, tossed the towel onto a chair and pulled on his slacks.

"Better?" he asked when he'd fastened the belt in place around them.

Better. She stared at him with pure pleasure, her eyes drifting over his broad, hair-covered chest down to his narrow waist and lean hips and long, powerful legs. He even had nice feet. She loved looking at him. But that was going to get her in trouble again so she averted her eyes to the bed.

He knew why. He sat back down with a long, heavy sigh and smoothed his big, warm hand over her bare shoulder. It was cool and damp to the touch. Her face was too pale, and a little pinched.

"Go ahead," he invited. "Look at me. It doesn't matter anymore. I suppose I told you all there was to tell last night. I don't remember too much of what I said, but I'm sure I was eloquent," he added bitterly.

She lifted her eyes warily to meet his. She didn't say anything, but her face was sad and resigned and without life.

He grimaced. "Barrie..."

She burrowed her face into the pillow and gripped it. "Leave me alone," she whispered miserably. "You've had what you wanted, and now you hate me all over again. It's always the same, it's always...!"

He had her up in his arms, close, bruisingly close. His face nuzzled against her soft throat through a cushion of thick wavy dark hair. "I love you," he said hoarsely. "I love you more than my own life! Damn it, isn't that enough?"

It was what he'd said last night, but he was sober now. She wanted so badly to believe it! But she didn't trust him. "You don't want to love me," she whimpered, clinging closer.

He sighed heavily, as if he was letting go of some intolerable burden. "Yes, I do," he said after a minute, and he sounded as if he were defeated. "I want you and our baby. I want to hold you in the darkness and make love to you in the light. I want to kiss away the tears and share the good times. But I'm afraid."

"Not you," she whispered, smoothing the hair at his nape. "You're strong. You don't feel fear."

"Only with you," he confessed. "Only *for* you. I never had a weakness until you came along." His arms contracted. "Barrie," he said hesitantly, "if I lose you, I can't live."

Her heart jumped. "But, you aren't going to lose me!" she said. "I'm not going to walk out on you. I didn't really mean it. I thought you wanted me to go."

"No!" he said huskily, lifting his head. He looked worried. Really worried. He traced her soft cheek. "That's not what I meant. I meant that I could lose you when you have the baby."

"Oh, for heaven's sake...!" she exclaimed, stunned.

"Women do still die in childbirth," he muttered uncomfortably . "My mother...did."

She was learning things about him that she would never have dared ask, that she hadn't known at all. She searched his eyes slowly. "Your mother died in childbirth?"

He nodded. "She was pregnant. She didn't want to be, and she tried to have an abortion, but my father found out and made so many threats about cutting off the money she liked to spend that she gave in. She went into labor and something went wrong. They were out of the country, on a trip she'd insisted on taking even that late in her pregnancy. The only medical care available was at a small clinic. It was primitive, there was only an intern there at the time." He sighed heavily. "And she died. He loved her, just as he'd loved your mother. It took him years to get over it. He felt responsible. So would I, if something happened to you."

Her fingers twined around his. It was humbling to realize that he loved her that much. He didn't want to get rid of her at all. He'd gone to the other extreme. He was terrified that he might lose her.

"I'm strong and healthy and I want this baby. I want to live," she said softly. "I couldn't leave you, Dawson," she added firmly. "Not even to die."

He looked down into her wet eyes and his face was strained, taut. He looked so stoic and immovable that it shocked her when he traced her mouth with a finger that wasn't quite steady.

"You'll learn to trust me one day," she said softly. "You'll learn that I'll never deliberately hurt you, or belittle you, or try to make you feel less of a man because you care about me. And our child will never be mocked or spoken to with sarcasm."

His hand stilled on her face. "And you won't leave me," he added with a bitter laugh.

She smiled. "No," she said gently. "I have no life without you." She took his hand and slid it under the cover to lie on the soft, bare swell of her stomach. "I'm pregnant," she said. "We have a future to think about."

"A future." His hand flattened where she'd placed it. "I guess I'm going to have to stop living on bad memories. It's hard."

"The first step is to look ahead," she told him.

He shrugged. He began to smile. "I suppose so. How far ahead?"

"To the nearest department store," she said with sudden humor. "I can't spend the day without underwear!"

He pursed his lips and for the first time since she'd arrived, he looked relaxed. "Why not?" he asked. "Are you sore already?"

She stared up at him uncertainly.

"Are you?" he persisted, and his hand moved insinu-atingly. "Because I want to make love again."

"It's broad daylight," she said pointedly.

His broad shoulders rose and fell. "It was broad day-light a few minutes ago," he reminded her. His face was solemn. "You kept your eyes closed. Don't do it again. I won't make any more snide remarks about it. I'm sorry I made you ashamed of wanting to watch something so beautiful."

She wasn't sure how to take this apparent change in him. She searched his pale eyes, but there were no more secrets there. He wasn't hiding anything from her.

"I know," he murmured ruefully. "You don't quite trust me, either, do you? But we'll work it out."

"Can we?"

The knock at the door interrupted what he might have replied. Barrie quickly slipped on his shirt and buttoned it while he let the waiter in, signed the bill and handed the man a tip on his way out.

"Take that off," he murmured when he'd locked the door again, nodding toward the shirt.

"I won't," she replied.

"Yes, you will. But we'll let your stomach get settled first," he conceded. He picked up the small dish of homemade strawberry ice cream and sat down on the bed, lifting half a spoonful of it to her lips.

She was surprised, and looked it.

"You fed me when I had the wreck," he reminded her. "Turnabout is fair play."

"I'm not injured," she replied.

"Yes, you are," he said quietly. "Right here." He put the spoon into the hand holding the small crystal goblet and with his free hand he touched her soft breast through the shirt. He felt its immediate response, but he didn't follow up. He lifted the spoon again to her mouth. "Come on," he coaxed. "It's good for you."

She had a sudden picture of Dawson with a toddler, smiling just like that, coaxing food into a stubborn small mouth and she managed a watery smile as she took the ice cream.

"What are you thinking about?" he wondered.

"A little mouth that doesn't want medicine or spinach," she said quietly.

He understood her. His eyes darkened, but not with irritation. He took a long breath and held another spoonful of ice cream to her mouth. Eventually he smiled. "I guess I might as well learn to change diapers and give bottles, too," he mused softly.

"No bottles," she said firmly. "I want to nurse the baby."

His hand stilled halfway to her mouth. He searched her eyes, shocked at the way the statement aroused him.

She could tell from the tautness of his body and the darkness of his eyes, from the faint flush across his cheekbones what he was feeling. She felt her own breath catch in her throat. She could see him in her mind, watching as she nursed the baby...

"You're trembling," he said unsteadily.

She moved restlessly and a self-conscious laugh passed her lips. "I was thinking about you watching me with the baby," she said shyly.

"So was I."

She let her eyes fall to his hard mouth, tracing the firm, sensuous lips. She caught her breath as a wave of hunger swept over her body.

"Good God." He whispered it reverently. He set the goblet aside carefully, because his hands weren't steady. And when he turned back to her, she had the shirt open. She pulled the edges aside, red-faced and taut, and watched him as he looked at her hard-tipped breasts.

Shakily her hands went to his face and she tugged as she lay back on the bed, dragging his mouth to her breast. He suckled her hungrily, fiercely, pressing her back into the mattress with a pressure that was nothing short of headlong passion.

"I'm too hungry. I'll hurt you," he warned off, as he gave in to it.

"No, you won't." She drew him closer, arching under the heat of his mouth. "Oh, Dawson, Dawson, it's the sweetest sensation!"

"You taste of rose petals," he growled. "God, baby, I don't think I can hold it back this time!"

"It's all right," she repeated breathlessly. Her hands helped him get the fabric out of the way. She moved, fixed her body to his, helped him, guided him into sudden, stark intimacy. It should have been uncomfortable, but it wasn't.

He felt the ease of his possession and lifted his head to look into her eyes as he levered above her, softly kissing her. "I'll let you...watch," he whispered, shivering as he felt the tension building in his loins. "I don't mind. I love you. I love you, Barrie. I love you...!"

She watched his face tauten, the flush that spread to his cheekbones as his eyes began to dilate and the movements quickened into fierce, stark passion. He lifted his chest away from hers, his teeth clenched.

"Look..." he managed before he lost control completely.

Barrie went with him every step of the way. She lifted to the harsh, violent demand of his body for the satisfaction hers could give it. She opened herself to him, clung to him, as he cried out in great shuddering waves of ecstasy. Then she, too, cried out as her body exploded into pulsing shards of exquisite color, burning so high from the pleasure that the whole world spun around her.

His voice came from far away and it sounded concerned. "What's wrong?" he asked gently.

"I'm fine." Her eyes opened, wide and green and dazed with satiation. She traced the whorls of damp hair on his body. "I said the most shocking things," she said uncomfortably.

"Wicked, sexy things," he agreed. He smiled. "I loved it."

"Oh."

He bent and brushed his mouth over hers. "There shouldn't be limits on what we can say to each other in bed, what we can do to each other," he explained gently. "I won't ever tease you about it."

"That goes for me, too." She searched his face. "I watched you," she whispered.

He flushed. "I know. I wanted you to."

She smiled self-consciously. "But I couldn't really see much," she added shyly. "Stars were exploding in my head."

"That was mutual. And I couldn't really watch you for the same reason." He chuckled. "I suppose I'm losing my inhibitions, bit by bit."

"Maybe I am, too." She pushed back his damp hair gently. "I like being intimate with you. I like feeling you as close as you can get to me."

He drew her close and rolled onto his back with a long sigh. "Intimacy is new to me," he revealed.

She hit him. "Ha! Where did you learn all those things you did to me this morning? No!" She put her hand over his mouth. "No, don't you tell me, I don't want to know!"

He lifted her onto his chest and searched her angry eyes. "Yes, you do. And I'm going to tell you. I learned them with a succession of carefully chosen, emotionally alienated one-night stands. I learned them without any real participation except for a superficial one. No, don't look away. You're going to hear this." He turned her flushed face back to his. "I have had sex. But until I touched your body, I had never made love. That day on the floor of my study was the first time in my life that I gave myself completely and deliberately to a woman.''

She felt hot all over. "You didn't like it."

"I loved it," he said harshly. "I didn't like having you watch it happen to me. I didn't trust you enough." His eyes calmed. "I'm sorry about that, too. We made a baby in the heat of that exquisite loving. I'm sorry I didn't make it a happier memory for you . . . for both of us."

"I'm not sorry about the baby. Or about watching you," she whispered wickedly. "It was the most exciting, embarrassing thing that ever happened to me."

"I can imagine," he replied quietly. "Because I kept my head long enough to watch you this morning, all through it." His eyes began to glitter. "And now I understand why you had to see my face."

She eased down over his chest and kissed him softly, nibbling his upper lip. "Because you wanted to see the love in my eyes," she whispered.

"Yes. And that's what you saw in mine, above and beyond the desire that was making me helpless, wasn't it?" he asked.

She nodded after a minute. "I didn't recognize it at the time. But, yes it was. It was the love that you didn't want me to see," she realized.

"Yes." He traced her nose with his forefinger, enjoying the lazy intimacy of their sprawled bodies. "I could have saved myself the trouble. You honestly didn't know how I felt until I told you in a drunken rage last night, did you?"

"No, I didn't," she confessed with a chuckle. "And it knocked me so hard that I got on the first plane out here to see if you meant it." She glared at him. "I thought you didn't want me here."

"I was surprised that you came, and delighted at being spared the trouble of flying right out to Sheridan to show you how completely I'd given in to my own feelings toward you."

Her body lay open to his eyes, and he looked at her with wonder and obvious pleasure. "I couldn't even do this before, did you realize it?" he asked quietly. "It made me feel uncomfortable to see you nude, to look at you openly."

"Then we're making progress."

"Apparently." He traced around her taut nipple and frowned as he saw the blue veins that had become prominent. The nipple was darker, bigger. His hand slid down to her belly and he felt the thickening of her waist. A smile pulled up the corners of his mouth. "My, how you're changing."

She smiled complacently. "I'll be as big as a pumpkin by Christmas."

His hand caressed her. "So you will." He bent and drew his mouth gently over her stomach. "We didn't hurt him, did we?"

"Babies are very tough," she said. She knew he was remembering the one they'd lost. "This one wants to be born," she added. "I feel it."

He lifted his head and searched her eyes. He didn't say anything for a long time. His eyes said all too much.

"You won't lose me," she said deliberately. "I promise you won't."

He took a long breath and let it out. "Okay."

She sat up, pressing close to him. "I'm sleepy."

"So am I. I think a nap might be a good idea. Do you feel better?"

"Oh, yes. I didn't ever feel bad," she murmured with a chuckle. "On the contrary, I felt entirely too good."

He drew her closer. "So did I. I wonder if two people ever achieved such a high at the same time?"

"Should we call the people at the record book and ask . . . ouch!"

He'd pinched her behind. He chuckled at her outraged expression. "I'll repent. Come here. We'll sleep for a while."

"A while?" she teased as he ensconced them together under the sheet.

His hand cradled her belly. "Life can be sweet after all."

"Hmmm," she murmured drowsily. Her eyes closed. She went to sleep with the sound of Dawson's heart beating softly at her ear.

Twelve

The phone was ringing off the hook. Barrie opened her eyes, disoriented. The phone was on the bedside table, on the other side of a broad, very hairy chest. She stared at that chest for a moment trying to get her bearings. Then she remembered where she was.

She smiled as she poked him in the ribs and felt him jump, coming awake immediately.

"Phone," she said, shaking him gently.

He reached over and picked it up. "Rutherford," he said shortly. He was quiet for a moment, then he rolled over onto his back and ran a hand through his hair. "What?" he said then. He made a rough sound in his throat. "Hell, no! Good God, man, what sort of person do you think I am?" There was the sound of hurried, apologetic conversation. "You'd damn well better apologize, if you expect me to stay here again or book my people in for another conference. You didn't? Well, that's no excuse. Yes, I should think you are! Very well." He slammed the receiver down and then started laughing.

"What was that all about?" she asked curiously.

He rolled onto his side to prop on his elbow and looked down at her. "It seems that the prestige of the hotel was briefly lowered when one of the guests threw a woman's dress and very skimpy underwear out of a window. Naturally I had no idea why they should suspect me of... Stop that!" He flicked her cheek with a long forefinger when she started laughing. "You have no idea who did it, either. Remember that. I spend a lot of time here when I travel, and I do want to come back again."

"I still can't believe you threw my clothes out the window!"

He grinned. "It seemed the best way to keep you from leaving." He lifted the sheet and looked at her with eyes as appreciative as any artist's. He shook his head. "God almighty," he breathed. "I've never seen anything so beautiful."

She grinned back. "Lecher."

He drew her against him and held her close with a long, lazy sigh as his legs tangled softly with hers. "Sore?"

"Very."

"So am I," he confessed, chuckling at her expression. "Men aren't made of iron, you know."

"No kidding!"

His arms tightened. "I suppose we'll have beautiful memories for the next few days, at least."

"Several." She touched the faint cleft in his chin gently. "Dawson, I can't go back to Sheridan naked."

"You can't?"

She hit him.

"All right. I'll go shopping." He grinned wickedly. "How about a maternity dress?"

"I don't even show yet," she scoffed.

"Why waste time wearing normal clothes until you do?" he wanted to know. "A man has his pride, Barrie. I'm rather anxious to show off what I've accomplished in such a short time."

Her eyebrows lifted. "*I'm* an accomplishment?!"

"By God, you are," he said huskily. "The most wonderful accomplishment of my life, you and this baby. I must have a guardian angel sitting on my shoulder."

She slid her arms around his neck and reached over to kiss him lazily. "Then so must I, I guess, because you're certainly my most wonderful accomplishment."

He searched her loving eyes with pride and a lingering sense of wonder. "I'm sorry it took me so long to deal with the past," he said. "I wish I'd told you when you were sixteen that I was going to love you obsessively when you were old enough."

Her eyes twinkled. "Did you know so long ago?"

"Part of me must have," he replied, and he was serious as he searched her green eyes. "I was violent about you from the very beginning."

"And I never even suspected why," she agreed. She smoothed her hand over his thick gold hair, tracing the wave that fell onto his broad forehead. "What would have become of us if you hadn't dragged me back to Sheridan to act as chaperone for you and Leslie Holton?"

"I'd have found another excuse to get you home."

"Excuse?"

"I've been managing flirtatious women for a lot longer than five years, honey," he said with a deliberate grin.

"You said you were desperate to get that land!"

"I was desperate to get *you* home," he replied lazily. "There's another tract of land on the north end of the property that's just become available, and I bought it before Powell Long even had time to get a bid in. I didn't need Leslie's tract anymore. Of course, she didn't know that. Neither did you."

"I'm in awe of you," she said, aghast.

He lifted a rakish eyebrow. "That's just right. A woman should always be in awe of her husband."

"And a man in awe of his wife," she returned pertly.

He grinned. "I'm in awe of you, all right."

"Good. I'll do my best to keep you that way."

He stretched drowsily and drew her close. "We can sleep a bit longer. Then we should go home."

"I didn't leave labels in any of my clothes," she pointed out. "The ones you threw out the window, I mean. There's no way they could identify you as the mystery lingerie tosser."

"That's not why I want to go home. It's been just about six weeks, hasn't it? And despite the home pregnancy test, I want proof. I want something I can take up on the roof and wave at people."

She nuzzled her cheek against his chest. "You'll get it," she promised.

And he did. The doctor confirmed not only that Barrie was pregnant, but that she was disgustingly healthy and should be over her morning sickness in no time.

As she and Dawson settled down in Sheridan, she thought back over the long, lonely years they'd been apart and how wonderful it was to have their future settled so comfortably.

Dawson was still sensitive to teasing just at first, but as he and Barrie grew together he became less defensive, more caring, more tender. Over the months of her pregnancy, Dawson was as attentive and supportive as any prospective mother could wish her husband to be. He seemed to have finally dealt with all his fears, even the one of childbirth.

But the most incredible revelation Barrie was ever to see was the look on Dawson's handsome face when he held their twin sons in his arms. As he looked into her worn,

delighted face, the expression in his pale green eyes would
last her the rest of her life. He looked as if he had the
world in that small hospital room. And, as he later told
Barrie, he did!

*   *   *   *   *

Don't miss these additional titles by favorite author
DIANA PALMER!

Silhouette Desire®

#05733	+THE CASE OF THE MISSING SECRETARY	$2.89	☐
#05829	*SECRET AGENT MAN	$2.99	☐
#05913	THAT BURKE MAN	$3.25 U.S.	☐
		$3.75 CAN.	☐

+Most Wanted series
*Man of the Month

Silhouette Romance™

#19000	REGAN'S PRIDE	$2.75	☐
#19103	COLTRAIN'S PROPOSAL	$2.99 U.S.	☐
		$3.50 CAN.	☐

By Request™

#20112	LONG, TALL TEXANS II	$5.50 U.S.	☐
		$5.99 CAN.	☐

TOTAL AMOUNT	$
POSTAGE & HANDLING ($1.00 for one book, 50¢ for each additional)	$
APPLICABLE TAXES**	$_____
TOTAL PAYABLE	$_____
(check or money order—please do not send cash)	

To order, complete this form and send it, along with a check or money order for the total above, payable to Silhouette Books, to: **In the U.S.:** 3010 Walden Avenue, P.O. Box 9077, Buffalo, NY 14269-9077; **In Canada:** P.O. Box 636, Fort Erie, Ontario, L2A 5X3.

Name:_____

Address:_____City:_____

State/Prov.:_____ Zip/Postal Code:_____

**New York residents remit applicable sales taxes.
Canadian residents remit applicable GST and provincial taxes.   SDPBACK12

Silhouette®
™

MILLION DOLLAR SWEEPSTAKES
AND EXTRA BONUS PRIZE DRAWING

No purchase necessary. To enter the sweepstakes, follow the directions published and complete and mail your Official Entry Form. If your Official Entry Form is missing, or you wish to obtain an additional one (limit: one Official Entry Form per request, one request per outer mailing envelope) send a separate, stamped, self-addressed #10 envelope (4 1/8" x 9 1/2") via first class mail to: Million Dollar Sweepstakes and Extra Bonus Prize Drawing Entry Form, P.O. Box 1867, Buffalo, NY 14269-1867. Request must be received no later than January 15, 1998. For eligibility into the sweepstakes, entries must be received no later than March 31, 1998. No liability is assumed for printing errors, lost, late, non-delivered or misdirected entries. Odds of winning are determined by the number of eligible entries distributed and received.

Sweepstakes open to residents of the U.S. (except Puerto Rico), Canada and Europe who are 18 years of age or older. All applicable laws and regulations apply. Sweepstakes offer void wherever prohibited by law. Values of all prizes are in U.S. currency. This sweepstakes is presented by Torstar Corp., its subsidiaries and affiliates, in conjunction with book, merchandise and/or product offerings. For a copy of the Official Rules governing this sweepstakes, send a self-addressed, stamped envelope (WA residents need not affix return postage) to: MILLION DOLLAR SWEEP-STAKES AND EXTRA BONUS PRIZE DRAWING Rules, P.O. Box 4470, Blair, NE 68009-4470, USA.

SWP-ME96

SILHOUETTE DESIRE® "CELEBRATION 1000" SWEEPSTAKES
OFFICIAL RULES—NO PURCHASE NECESSARY

To enter, complete an Official Entry Form or a 3"x5" card by hand printing "Silhouette Desire Celebration 1000 Sweepstakes," your name and address, and mail it to: In the U.S.: Silhouette Desire Celebration 1000 Sweepstakes, P.O. Box 9069, Buffalo, NY 14269-9069, or In Canada: Silhouette Desire Celebration 1000 Sweepstakes, P.O. Box 637, Fort Erie, Ontario L2A 5X3. Limit one entry per envelope. Entries must be sent via first-class mail and be received no later than 6/30/96. No liability is assumed for lost, late or misdirected mail.

Prizes: Grand Prize—an original painting (approximate value $1500 U.S.);300 Runner-up Prizes—an autographed Silhouette Desire® Book (approximate value $3.50 U.S./$3.99 CAN. each). Winners will be selected in a random drawing (to be conducted no later than 9/30/96) from among all eligible entries received by D.L. Blair, Inc., an independent judging organization whose decision is final.

Sweepstakes offer is open only to residents of the U.S. (except Puerto Rico) and Canada who are 18 years of age or older, except employees and immediate family members of Harlequin Enterprises Ltd., their affiliates, subsidiaries, and all agencies, entities and persons connected with the use, marketing or conduct of this sweepstakes. All federal, state, provincial, municipal and local laws apply. Offer void where prohibited by law. Taxes and/or duties are the sole responsibility of the winners. Any litigation within the province of Quebec respecting the conduct and awarding of prizes may be submitted to the Regie des alcools des courses et des jeux. All prizes will be awarded; winners will be notified by mail. No substitution for prizes is permitted. Odds of winning are dependent upon the number of eligible entries received.

Grand Prize winner must sign and return an Affidavit of Eligibility within 30 days of notification. In the event of noncompliance within this time period, prize may be awarded to an alternate winner. Any prize or prize notification returned as undeliverable may result in the awarding of that prize to an alternate winner. By acceptance of their prize, winners consent to the use of their names, photographs or likenesses for purposes of advertising, trade and promotion on behalf of Harlequin Enterprises Ltd., without further compensation unless prohibited by law. In order to win a prize, residents of Canada will be required to correctly answer a time-limited arithmetical skill-testing question administered by mail.

For a list of winners (available after October 31, 1996) send a separate self-addressed stamped envelope to: Silhouette Desire Celebration 1000 Sweepstakes Winners, P.O. Box 4200, Blair, NE 68009-4200.

SWEEPR

Who can resist a Texan...or a Calloway?

This September, award-winning author
ANNETTE BROADRICK
returns to Texas, with a brand-new
story about the Calloways...

SONS OF TEXAS
Rogues and Ranchers

CLINT: The brave leader. Used to keeping secrets.

CADE: The Lone Star Stud. Used to having women
fall at his feet...

MATT: The family guardian. Used to handling
trouble...

They must discover the identity of the mystery
woman with Calloway eyes—and uncover a
conspiracy that threatens their family....

Look for **SONS OF TEXAS:** Rogues and Ranchers
in September 1996!

Only from Silhouette...where passion lives.

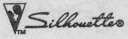

In July, get to know the Fortune family....

Next month, don't miss the start of Fortune's Children, a fabulous new twelve-book series from Silhouette Books.

Meet the Fortunes—a family whose legacy is greater than riches. Because where there's a will...there's a wedding!

When Kate Fortune's plane crashes in the jungle, her family believes that she's dead. And when her will is read, they discover that Kate's plans for their lives are more interesting than they'd ever suspected.

Look for the first book, *Hired Husband*, by *New York Times* bestselling author **Rebecca Brandewyne.** PLUS, a stunning, perforated bookmark is affixed to *Hired Husband* (and selected other titles in the series), providing a convenient checklist for all twelve titles!

FREE
Keepsake
Bookmark

Launching in July wherever books are sold.

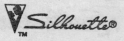

You're About to Become a

Privileged Woman

Reap the rewards of fabulous free gifts and benefits with proofs-of-purchase from Silhouette and Harlequin books

Pages & Privileges™

It's our way of thanking you for buying our books at your favorite retail stores.

Pages & Privileges ™

Harlequin and Silhouette—
the most privileged readers in the world!

For more information about Harlequin and Silhouette's PAGES & PRIVILEGES program call the Pages & Privileges Benefits Desk: 1-503-794-2499